EVER AFTER

BOOK 4

BEAUTY AND THE BEAST

NIKKI DEAN

Beauty and the Beast pt. 4
FRISKY FAIRY TALES

UNTITLED

This book is dedicated to Sally Poe, for being as exuberant and enthusiastic as I occasionally needed her to be, and to my husband, who encouraged me to just keep trucking even when I was exhausted.

1

Belle couldn't breathe. Shock rendered her speechless, her throat closing as she struggled to make sense of what she was seeing.

But how is this possible? He was cursed. Never to be human again, and he told me that he couldn't leave the castle or he'd get sick. Ian was never sick, and he was most definitely human!

Her chest clenched as she thought of the letters, conversations, and worst of all, the kisses that she'd shared with Ian. Kisses that she'd never told Beast about because she was afraid he wouldn't understand.

*He knew the whole time, because it was **him**! Was this all some kind of sick game?!* Belle flung herself backwards, barely getting her hands behind her in time. Scooting off of his lap, she landed on her backside with a thump, then shoved at him with her slippered feet, propelling herself across the floor.

"What's going on here, *Beast*? Or do you prefer Ian, instead?" she hissed at him. "Was this all some kind of game to you? To make me fall in love with you here, then see how far you could get as a man?"

He flinched. "Of course not, Belle. It's – complicated." He reached out to her, then let his hands drop as she scooted farther away, glaring.

"Well, I suggest you figure out how to uncomplicate it! You've been keeping secrets from me the entire time I've known you, and now this?! You lied to me, Beast!"

And now that you're human again, you'll have to go be the king. Soul-deep sorrow grew to match the anger in her heart. She shoved it aside for later.

"Tell me everything," Belle demanded.

"Are you sure?" he asked, looking away. "I'm so afraid that you'll hate me."

"Keeping secrets from me now will only ensure it," she retorted.

Happy laughter and cheers filtered down the hallway and through the closed dining room door. The sounds were coming closer.

"I'll tell you everything tonight. I promise. But please, just give me a moment with them, too? They were cursed because of me, and none of them thought they'd ever be human again, either. Is there any way that you can just trust that I love you, and would never hurt you?" Ian nearly begged.

He crawled to her, crouching in front of her outstretched legs. "Please, Belle. I love you so damn much, and I'm sorrier than I can ever say for all of the pain that I've caused you. You're my world now, and I hate myself for making you cry."

But that doesn't mean you have to stay when you're supposed to be ruling the entire country. I'm not a princess, she thought. *Love doesn't solve everything, and you're already trying to go be with your servants instead of helping me understand. I'm not putting up with this anymore.*

"I love you, too," she whispered back. "But that doesn't

mean that I'll accept being left out anymore. You have to tell me everything, now. And I mean *everything*." She let him pull her close.

"I will, I promise." He crushed her against his chest and held her tightly. "Just don't leave me after you know the whole story."

"Why would I?" Burying her face against him, she took a deep breath to calm herself. His shirt still smelled like Beast, comforting her. Intrigued, she stretched up and nuzzled into his throat, wanting to find out if he smelled the same, too.

He didn't.

But I want my Beast, she thought with a twinge of regret.

Ian shuddered. "That feels so good, Belle. My skin – it's so sensitive now that the fur is gone. Everything is so much more intense now."

Belle bit her lip as she dropped her head back down to his shoulder. All of her previous enthusiasm had fled, leaving her unsure of what to do next.

"You didn't have to stop," he said into her hair.

"I just – it'll take me a little while to get used to." *If I ever do. You'd better have a damn good reason for deceiving me as Ian, or I'm not certain I'll ever touch you again.* The conviction in her thoughts surprised her, even if she didn't voice it aloud.

"Start talking," Belle demanded. "Why did you lie to me about becoming human?"

"I didn't mean to. I honestly didn't know it would happen the first time, then I couldn't say anything for so many different reasons. Not least of which was that the enchantress promised the curse would become permanent, and I wasn't sure if my occasional reprieves counted. They weren't exactly included in her terms."

Someone pounded on the door. Mrs. Ambly's cheerful

voice rose on the other side, ordering Etienne to leave them alone.

"If it wasn't included, then how on earth did you manage to turn back into a man? And how often?" Belle demanded. *And how many women did you dally with during these so-called reprieves?* Corinne's shrewd eyes sliding away as she said she used to be close to Ian and the barmaid pulling him back into Gustav's tavern flashed through Belle's mind.

"Have you been with anyone else since I moved to the castle?" she blurted, unable to keep the words from flying out of her mouth.

"*What?!*" He grabbed her shoulders and pulled her away from his chest. Incredulous, his mouth hung open for a moment before he could continue. "Christ, Belle, I just *proposed* to you! Then told you how much I love you, which apparently almost killed me and released my entire household from a decade-long curse, and now you're asking if I've been unfaithful?! Is that what you really think of me?"

His tight grip and eyes sparkling with anger actually soothed the turmoil within her. "No. But I still felt like I had to ask. I saw that barmaid hanging on you in the tavern yesterday morning." *And Corinne may as well have told me that she'd been intimate with you, even if she didn't say when.*

"Of course not! I was only in that tavern because it was close to the bookstore, and after what you'd said about me not having any idea what I wanted from a woman, it seemed like a good spot to think."

"Because of all of the easy women there?" Belle raised an eyebrow.

He blushed. "It's exactly the kind of place I used to frequent before the curse. I wanted to see if I could figure out why I enjoyed it so much, and if there really is something wrong with me."

"And? What did you think?"

He swallowed hard, looking a bit ill. "I hated it."

She snorted. "It didn't look that way to me."

"No, really. I wished you were there the whole time. My skin crawled every time that waitress touched me."

"You didn't look very upset about it when I saw you. You even let her pull you back in."

"Because I hadn't paid my tab, and I needed to keep up appearances if I ever had a hope of spending time with you in your village again."

Belle frowned. "Why would that matter? I didn't plan on ever going back there, once Papa's workshop burned down."

"How could I have known that? I thought that those few hours every solstice were the only chance I'd get to see you, touch you, spend time with you, as a man. I didn't know you were leaving for good, and didn't believe the curse would ever be broken."

"*Touch me?!*" she repeated in shock. "You honestly thought that I'd let some other man into my life when I had my Beast at home?" It was her turn to pull away in angry disgust. "You really don't know me at all, do you? How could you love me, believing that I'd eventually be unfaithful to you, with, well, you?"

She stood, straightening her skirts as she marched toward the door. "You really don't value the intimacy between us if you thought that I regarded it so casually. Ian was never going to get to touch me like that again, and I honestly don't know if you will either, now."

A very Beast-like growl stopped her in her tracks. Belle turned to find him upon her, glowering as he snatched her back against him and dropped his mouth onto hers.

The kiss was everything. Molten heat poured through her, searing her from the top of her head down to her toes, and sending trembles racing down her back. He nipped at her lips as he teased them open, then swept inside. It was everything good about kissing Beast, with none of his former caution to slow them down.

I know he loves me, or the curse wouldn't have broken. Surely it can't be wrong to just enjoy it, right? she wondered. *Even if it ends up being just this once?*

Ian groaned as Belle lost herself in the embrace, melting against him. Her lush curves molding to his larger frame, he sank back into the chair from earlier. She stiffened at first, still upset, but relaxed as he kept kissing her.

Their lips met again and again, and goosebumps broke out over her skin as he smoothed her hair back to cup the back of her head. It was gentle, but still demanding enough to bring her to life.

Ian pulled her higher in his lap, stroking her back and finally her rear end as he squeezed it with a growl. She couldn't hold back a little moan.

Belle's knees opened, straddling his lap like she had so many times before.

Ian grabbed her hips and rocked her against his erection, grinding up into her center. Her skirt pulled tight over her thighs, barely keeping her from him.

"Belle, my love, I need you to lift a little. I can't get this up," he growled between kisses. He clenched her skirt in his hands, cursing the awkward position and lesser strength of his new form.

"What?" she pulled back, dazed. "Lift?"

Ian grabbed a fistful of her skirt and jerked it upward, nearly knocking her out of his lap. She grabbed onto the chair's arms to steady herself.

"Oh, that. No, wait." Belle sat back down, keeping the

garment trapped between them. The lust-filled haze was already fading from her expression.

Damn it all to hell. Ian groaned.

"I'm sorry," he muttered. "I got carried away. I've been waiting so long to do this with you as a man, and didn't think it would ever really be possible."

"But you just said you were keeping up appearances so you could touch me as Ian." Belle's eyes narrowed. "Explain."

2

He threaded his fingers through hers and pulled her hand to his mouth. "Touch your hand, your arm, maybe occasionally your hair, if you let me. Just normal affection between friends. Not even kissing anymore, although I was definitely disappointed when I thought I'd lost that, too." He sighed. "It was extremely hard for me to accept that you could ever love me as the beast. You know that. So when I first introduced myself to you as Ian, I had this stupid idea that you might develop some affection for me as a man, and I could just visit you every three months. We could stay connected and get to know each other through letters, and spend whatever time together we could once I transformed."

Ian shook his head. "It was foolish. But I didn't dare hope for anything else from you. Certainly not love, in either form."

Belle stared at him, baffled. "So your whole plan was to kiss me senseless the first time we met, then write me letters while you were supposedly on your merchant circuit, and what? Ignore me as the beast? I was living here with you, for goodness' sake. How could you not think that we'd get close? Especially with you trying to seduce me every chance you got?"

He blushed as he shrugged. "Like I said, it was a stupid idea. I just knew that I'd had this taste of you at dinner that first night, and I couldn't resist more. I thought you'd get tired of being here and leave, or get frightened away. There was no way I could have followed you because of the limitations the curse kept on me. I regret it now, of course, but I couldn't tell you, and the temptation of even escorting you home from the bookstore like a regular man was more than I could resist."

Her glare didn't fade.

"I'm sorry, Belle. I know it was wrong of me, but I wanted any scrap of normalcy with you that I could get. Even as just your merchant friend that was helping your father with his inventions. The sensation of just walking with you in the open air, surrounded by people and watching you smile, was magic."

"And you never planned to tell me?" The hurt in her voice was evident.

He sighed as he leaned his forehead against her chest. Her heart pounded and he smiled, relieved that he could still affect her. *Maybe there's still hope after all.*

"I knew you'd find out eventually. Either someone would let it slip, or you'd see one of the servants on a solstice. Or you'd find one of the paintings in my room and recognize me. I just hoped that you'd understand."

"See one of the servants, or they'd let it slip?" Belle repeated. "So everyone knew about this but me?!"

Ian flinched.

"Were you all just laughing at me behind my back? Can I not trust anyone here to tell me the truth?" She struggled to pull away from him.

Ian wrapped one arm around her waist, keeping her in his lap. "Don't be angry at them. It's my fault that no one told you – I expressly forbade it. It was just pure dumb luck that you didn't see the very first time, anyway. I had no idea that I could transform anymore, so it never occurred to me to mention it, even if I could have."

"What do you mean?"

He lifted her hand to his lips, absently running them along her knuckles. "I had been losing myself to the beast for such a long time before you came along. Years, Belle. I used to shift every solstice, back when the curse was first set, but it stopped after a while. We all went years without even seeing another human being, then when you showed up with your bravery and compassion, you reminded me what it was like to be a man again. To want to be something other than a monster."

Ian had to stop a moment, shaken by how close he'd actually come to losing himself. "Your light was strong enough to pull me back from darkness, and when you did, it allowed the magic of the second spell to take effect again. You saved us all, Belle. Not just me."

"What second spell? I swear, Beast, if you keep making me ask questions, I'm going to scream. Start at the beginning and tell me everything."

He released her waist and sat back. "It's a long story. Are you comfortable?"

Belle ground her teeth together in frustration. "Talk."

"I told you a little about how I grew up, and my experience with women. I regret to say that you're completely correct – I did take them for granted. A lot. And that continued until the day that the enchantress broke into this castle and stole everything from me."

"She claimed to be doing it because a girl came to her. Her name was Alison and I'd met her at a tavern. One thing led to another and we had sex, but I didn't know until it was too late that it was her first time. She's the only virgin I've ever been with, until you."

Belle swallowed hard. "Why not?"

Shrugging, Ian sighed. "I didn't like the innocence. I couldn't stand it, actually. I was just looking for a good time, and wanted women who were after the same thing. I never saw the draw in being someone's first – that one they always remember, good or bad. It just seemed like too much emphasis for me. Much better to just be a quick roll in the sack that a girl would have fun talking about later, instead of pining after."

He actually cares what people think of him, no matter what he'd like to say. He didn't want to take anything from anyone but me. "Why me?" she asked. "You've always known I'm a virgin, but that didn't stop you."

"My Belle. I don't think anything could have stopped me where you're concerned. You've opened my eyes in so many ways, one of them being that I'm glad you're so innocent. Grateful, even. It drives me insane to think about you being intimate with another man, even before we met, and I'm glad that you weren't. It's been so amazing to be your first. I'm selfish about everything about you."

He smiled as he reached up, trailing his fingertips along her collarbone. Goosebumps followed in their wake. "Like that. I love affecting you. I don't know if you'd be so responsive if someone else had done it before me, but I love that this is how you react when I touch you."

She stiffened. "Are you saying that you don't react like

that to me because you've been with so many other women? That I need to find myself a virgin man to get the same satisfaction?"

He snapped his teeth together, reminding her very much of her Beast. *I won't ever get to see him like that again, will I?* Unexpected loss filled her at the thought. *Never get to stroke his soft fur, or watch him flick his ears or feel his tail flipping against my leg while he sleeps. He even sounds different. I have to get to know this version all over again. I wish I'd said goodbye better.*

"Never, Belle. You affect me more than anyone I've ever been with. It might even be more intense because I have so many underwhelming experiences to compare it to. I know how precious this is between us."

"Then stop with this virgin nonsense."

He barked a little laugh. "You never fail to surprise me, you know that?" Leaning forward again, he nuzzled her throat.

He's always done that, Belle thought. *Maybe it won't be so very different, and I just need to give it time. He's still my beloved.*

His lips brushed her skin. Familiar tingles radiated outward and she had to stop herself from pressing against him, seeking more.

"How were you able to transform into Ian and leave the castle?"

Ian bit her shoulder, right on her favorite spot. Belle arched against him, grabbing his hair with a gasp.

"Beast! You promised to explain!" She pulled his head back as he growled, a feral look in his eyes.

"You are still in there," she whispered. The beast's orangey light almost radiated from his eyes. "My Beast."

"Always, Belle. I'm still the same person. Even without

the horns." He winked at her. "But you're more than welcome to pull my hair instead."

"Pervert."

"You know you want to."

"We'll see about that. You still haven't told me how you managed to deceive me. Even if I decide for some silly reason to forgive you for it, I still want to know how."

He bared his teeth and she nearly smiled as she pictured her Beast. "No pouting. You're lucky I'm still sitting here instead of slapping you for keeping so much from me, and yet you are still trying to get under my skirts even now."

Shifting in the chair, Ian pulled her against his chest. Tucking her head under his chin, he wrapped his arms around her and sighed. "There. Now maybe I won't be as tempted to rip that dress off of you and start doing all of the things I've been fantasizing about."

Belle rolled her eyes, but couldn't contradict him. An old dream she'd had about Ian pushing Beast out of the way to lick her sex came to mind. *I wonder if it would feel the same? Probably not. But would it be as good as before?* she wondered. *Stop it. I'm not going to encourage him. He's lied to me too many times to count, even if he felt that he had to. It's time he started trusting me.*

"I went into a rage after the enchantress cursed me. I had been turned into a monster, my parents and brother were gone, all of the servants were panicking and I had no idea what to do about any of it. The enchantress had said that she'd traded Alison a life for a life when she destroyed mine, and I didn't think that there was any way to break the spell. I didn't think that I deserved to, honestly."

"Why not?" Belle whispered. *Here's the thing he's so afraid of telling me. Why he thinks I'll hate him.*

Ian took a deep breath. "Because I had abandoned Alison when she needed me the most. We'd only slept together that one time, and I always used a condom with anyone. But it broke with her, and I didn't know until too late."

"What's a condom?"

"A thin sheath that goes over a man's cock to catch his orgasm. It prevents a woman from getting pregnant."

But he said it broke. So was she... "You have a child?"

"No. Not anymore." He laid his cheek against her head and slowly rubbed it back and forth. "I mean, I don't know. She said she thought so, but the royal physician said it was much too soon to tell, and that it probably wasn't mine. I only spoke with Alison about it once when she told me that she might be carrying, but she wasn't sure. So I was waiting for proof that the babe even existed at all before I told my parents, or decided what to do. I'm not sure what I would have done if it was real, but I never got the chance to find out."

"What happened to her?"

"She died. Either the bitch killed her as payment for my curse, or she killed herself. There's no way to know."

"How?"

His arms tightened around her. "She drowned."

"Oh." *It's no wonder that he was so brash and a little terrifying when we first met. He really has been through a lot, and I bet that's part of why Felicity and the tub scared him so much. He hardly left me alone after that.* She slid her arms around his waist. "Nothing's going to happen to me, Beast."

"You don't know that," he argued. "I've lost so much. I couldn't handle losing you, too. I'm afraid that would truly make me into a monster."

She hugged him, hard. "Then I suppose you'll just have

to keep an eye on me and make sure, won't you?" *There's nowhere else I want to be anyway, even if I know he'll eventually have to go be the king. Or at least join Sam's court.*

"Always, Belle. For as long as you'll have me, and probably even after that."

3

"What happened next?" Belle asked after a moment. "Who did the second spell if the enchantress was so awful?"

"You're actually not going to believe this, but Granny Rousseau did."

"What?" Belle pulled away and sat up, her mouth hanging open as she stared at him. "Granny Rousseau? The same one that my sister is living with?"

Ian smiled. "That very one." He hooked a finger under her chin and lifted it, then ran it along the edge of her bottom lip. Belle had to fight the sudden urge to lick it, like he'd done to her so many times before.

I want to hear the rest of the story, and that would definitely distract him, she lectured herself. *Even though I'm starting to see everything a little clearer, and I suppose him coming to see me as Ian isn't so bad. It was only twice, and I hadn't decided anything about Beast the first time. The letters weren't even inappropriate, much to Daphne's disappointment. Shit. Daphne. I told Ronan that we'd use the mirror to check on her, although I'm sure she's fine.*

"Apparently Sam made it off of the estate in time and somehow ended up wandering around in her corner of the woods. She found him, took care of him until he confessed who he was and what had happened, then got him back to the king's council in the capital. She only left him after she made sure he was well looked after, and then she came looking for me."

His voice had lowered as Belle leaned forward, fascinated by this development. "What did you do when she got here?"

"Let's just say I didn't have the same reaction as when I found you," he said with a snort.

"You mean you didn't threaten to eat her?"

Ian laughed. "All right, maybe it was a similar reaction. But it would have been carried out completely differently." His fingers brushed the sensitive spot under her ear and trailed down her throat.

She blushed and pulled back, snapped out of it. "You really are a scoundrel, aren't you?"

"Maybe so. But all I know is that I'm about to say to hell with self-control if you keep looking at me like that. It's been too long since I tasted you and now that you're my fiancée, I think a little celebration is in order."

Mmm, yes. Heat flooded Belle's body at the thought, leaving her quivering in its wake. *It's been barely more than a week since I was home with Beast, but it feels like so much longer. Probably more like two since we've been intimate. But fiancée? Could he still possibly want to marry me, even though he'll be reinstated to the throne?*

Ian's eyes flashed, almost as though he could hear her thoughts. "Belle. Say something, or I'm not going to be able to hold back."

She ducked and leaned against his chest again, not

entirely ready to end the conversation for such activities yet. *This would have been so much easier if I'd just never met him as Ian. Why did everything have to get so complicated?* "As delightful as that sounds, I don't think I'm quite ready yet. I'm still trying to wrap my head around it all."

Silence reigned for a moment. "Is it because of that kiss on your front porch? Is that why you're having so much trouble with this?" he finally asked.

"Partly. More because I knew you as two separate people, and finding out that you're the same man is very disconcerting. I admit that I was attracted to Ian at first, but I worried so much about hurting Beast's feelings that I never even wanted to see Ian again. Now, I'm just finding out that I've agreed to marry him. You. And my Beast, also you, knew about that kiss all along. It must have been part of why you thought I would leave you, even though I never would have once I got to know you. It all seems very unfair when I look back on it. You were judging me as Beast for something I'd done with Ian before I'd had time to fall in love with you. With Beast, I mean."

Her brow wrinkled as she thought about all of the ins and outs of it. "It feels almost like I was being set up for failure, and then you were so surprised when I chose my Beast. Which also hurts my feelings. Do you think there's something wrong with me for preferring that form over your human one?"

"There could never be anything wrong with you. I understand how you must feel, and I'll try to make it up to you. I'm sorry that you would rather have me as I was, instead of how I've ended up."

He gave a short, humorless laugh. "It's almost funny. I thought my life was over when I turned into that thing, then I find an amazing, wonderful woman that I love and who loves me back enough to break the curse. But she prefers the monster over the prince. Life has an odd way of working out."

Flinching a little under his words, Belle sighed. "It's not that I prefer the monster to the prince." *Mostly.* "It's that I would have preferred meeting you for the first time as a human now. Versus you having lied to me about being a merchant and playing with my emotions. I'd have been delighted if this was our first meeting, prince or not, no matter what you looked like. You'd have just been my Beast. But now you're Beast and Ian, and that will take me a little time to process. And I think you know that, or you wouldn't have been so afraid to let me see your real face. I don't even know what to call you now."

He nodded as he absently rubbed her back. "I know. But like you said, we'll get through this. Right?" His eyes were questioning, almost afraid, as he tilted her chin up. "I want you to call me whatever you're comfortable with. My name doesn't matter to me anymore, just that you're the one saying it."

Their eyes met, her soft brown ones with his hazel green, and remained locked a moment.

"Of course. One way or another, everything will be all right. Just no more secrets. I don't think I could take any more." *He loves me. I love him. I can understand why he did what he did, even if I don't agree with it. No one has bothered him for years about the kingdom, so there's no way for them to even know that he's human again, right? Maybe I can keep him after all.*

He gave her a surprisingly chaste kiss before tucking her back against his chest. "No more secrets. So, back to the story. Granny Rousseau came to find me and it went about as well as you would expect. Crying servants, me as a beast alternating between destroying things and tripping over my own feet. I'm not sure which was worse - the incoordination or the sudden, insane amount of strength. It seemed like everything I touched shattered into pieces. I can't tell you how many times I was afraid I had murdered someone just by brushing up against a piece of furniture. It was enough to drive anyone insane."

"And then I accused you of being so heartless that you did it on purpose," she murmured. "I'm so sorry. I didn't realize."

"It's fine. You didn't know. The whole situation was bizarre, and I don't blame you for jumping to conclusions. I'm fairly certain that I had just threatened your life, so it's not exactly an illogical thought."

"You never would have hurt me, though."

Stiffening slightly, he rubbed his cheek over her hair again. "But I did. You've been hurt several times because of me. First your ankle, then the vase. You were almost drowned, for God's sake. And don't forget that I broke your heart, more than once. I haven't exactly been good for your well-being."

Belle poked him, hard, and smiled when he grunted.

"Don't be ridiculous. Twisting my ankle was an accident, and nothing that Felicity did was your fault. It would have been nice if you'd told me about sleeping with her before you were cursed, but there's nothing we can do about that now. It's been a little difficult adjusting, that's true, but I can understand most of your decisions. I don't agree with them, but I understand what you must have been thinking."

"You're too good to me."

Another poke, this time gentler. "And don't you forget it," she whispered. *He's been through so much that it's a miracle he hasn't lost his mind out here, either from the curse or the sheer loneliness of it all. It's a miracle they all haven't.*

"So, where do we go from here?" Belle asked. "It'll take me a while to get used to, but you're so much like my Beast that I don't think it will be long. You still have his habits and mannerisms."

"Ugh. Growling at people probably won't have the same effect now."

"I don't know, I kind of like it. But then, I always have."

He gave her a mocking half-growl, half-groan. "Don't say things like that unless you're willing to accept the consequences. I don't particularly want your first time to be on the dining room table, but if you insist, I can make it happen."

"As romantic as that sounds…" she trailed off with a giggle. "No, thank you. You did a fantastic job getting everything set up in here and it looks lovely, but I think I'd rather have a bed, my love."

He stilled. "My love. I like it."

Heat flushed her cheeks. "I do, too. Now then, where were we?"

"Discussing how I'm going to eat you alive on this table?" There was a hopeful note in his voice.

"No, silly Beast. You were telling me about Granny Rousseau showing up."

He gripped her hips, fingers digging into her soft flesh. "Was I?" He leaned down and grazed her shoulder with his lips, then his teeth. "Are you sure?"

"Fairly." Tremors raced down her spine as his lips moved to her throat, kissed along the front and paused to dip into the little hollow at her collarbone. Ian leaned her back over one arm and kissed his way down her chest.

"Beast, stop." Belle was nearly breathless as he cupped

one breast in his palm and ran his thumb over its tip. "Not yet. Tell me the rest of the story."

He tugged at her neckline and bit the swell of her breast. She arched against his mouth.

Lower, she silently begged, even as she struggled to regain control. *It's been so long. And everything feels so different now that he's admitted he loves me and transformed... not nearly as cautious as before. I have a feeling he's not going to be holding back anymore.*

Ian hooked a finger into the neckline of her dress and tugged it down, mere breaths away from exposing her nipple. He ran his fingertip over its taut peak, making her jump.

"Are you certain?" he asked as he did it again. "Once I get this dress down, there's no going back."

"Didn't we just talk about the virtues of my first bedding taking place in an actual bed?" she teased. "Surely we can go to our room without running into anyone in the gardens. And you can finish the story after."

Ian growled in approval, gave her breast one last squeeze and stood. Belle squeaked as he held her up against him, firmly gripping her rear.

"Ah, Belle. I've been dreaming about fucking you like this," he whispered in her ear. "Hook your ankles together behind my back."

"Like this?" She did as he asked and clenched his waist with her thighs. Their centers lined up perfectly.

"Exactly." Clenching one of her cheeks in each hand, he rubbed her sex up and down his hard cock. Belle moaned as it pressed against her clit.

"You're going to be lucky if I can make it to our room. I'm not going to let you out for a week," he promised. "Everyone else be damned, we've waited long enough for this."

"Actually, that's not going to work out for me." Ronan's voice broke their reverie. "Don't get me wrong, I understand wanting to keep your mate to yourself for a while, especially given the circumstances, but I need to find her sister. And you're the only one that can help me."

"Who the fuck are you?" Beast demanded. He dumped Belle into the chair and stood before it, fists raised. "What are you doing in my home?"

4

"ctually, I invited him," Belle said, cringing. "Although why he's in here right now, I don't know."

"Sure you do, princess. You said you'd have him use the mirror to find Daphne and Grayson, then I understand he proposed, shifted back to his true form and now you're about to get busy. But I need him to use the magic mirror to make sure she's all right, and I figure that now is better than interrupting you once you've actually gotten naked."

He glanced back toward the door. "I saved your woman's life today, Beast Prince. This is the least you could do to repay me. Plus, there are a few people out there that I don't think are willing to wait for you much longer, and I want to get this out of the way first."

"Saved your life? Belle, who is he?" Beast asked over his shoulder, refusing to take his eyes off the half-naked stranger in his dining room. "What's he talking about?"

She took a shaking breath and stood, coming around between them. "Beast, this is Ronan. He lives in the woods near Granny's house and is apparently in some sort of relationship with my sister. He saved Papa, Phoebe and I from being eaten by giant wolves on the way here, because he's their leader or something. Oh, and Grayson is his son."

"Grayson? The wolf pup you brought when you and Finn moved in?"

Belle nodded. "Ronan is a wolf, as well. Or at least, he can turn into one."

"He can turn into a wolf," Beast repeated slowly. "And Grayson is his son."

"Who should currently be with Daphne, but I can't find her. Can't smell her, track her, nothing. Or him, or Granny Rousseau." Ronan leaned against the wall and crossed his arms. "So I need you to find them for me."

"Granny's here."

"What?" Both Ronan and Belle looked at Beast in surprise, but Belle spoke first. "What's she doing here? Is Daphne with her?"

"And Grayson?"

"I assume he is. I didn't see Daphne. Granny has a little boy with her, but she didn't mention his name and I didn't ask. They just arrived yesterday."

"But Daphne isn't with her?" Belle frowned. "She left Papa's earlier this week and said she was going home. But no one has been in Granny's cottage for at least that long."

"The mirror is in our room. Stay here and we'll be back," Beast ordered. He grabbed Belle's hand and began to pull her toward the kitchen, intending to use the back door.

"I'm coming with you. Like I said, there are a few people out there that are impatiently waiting, and I've a feeling you won't make it back this way any time soon."

"What's that supposed to mean?" Beast growled. "If you have friends out there causing trouble, I'll -"

"What? Eat them? Rip them apart?" Ronan scoffed.

"Your curse is broken, and your beast is gone. You're just a man now."

Do they already know, somehow? Belle began to panic. *Has someone come to take him to the capital and make him claim the throne?*

"I'm still the lord of this castle," Beast retorted. "Don't think that you can come in here and threaten my family-"

"I'm not threatening anyone," Ronan cut him off again. "I'm just letting you know that the whole hall is full of people waiting to see you. I didn't catch any names, but an older man and woman were particularly anxious."

"Mrs. Ambly and Etienne, I suppose," Belle murmured as she set her hand on Beast's arm. "Let's just let him come along. It'll be faster that way."

"If the mirror even works," Beast muttered. "Granny Rousseau is the one that gave it to me when she finally cast the spell that would allow me to transform back into a man every solstice. She pitied me because she couldn't break the curse outright, but wanted to give me some kind of window to the outside world."

"That was very kind of her," Belle replied as he pulled her toward the kitchen. Ronan trailed behind, keeping his distance.

Peeking out the backdoor, Ian grabbed the waistband of his too-large pants and began to jog, forcing Belle to lift her skirts and run after him. They made it to her balcony without being seen.

"Stay here," Ian ordered. Ronan sat in one of the outdoor chairs and stretched his long legs out in front of him.

"Don't think that I won't come in there if you decide to take too long," Ronan threatened. "I'm not saying that I want to see your naked ass waving around in the air, but I'm not letting it keep me from finding Daphne. I have a bad feeling."

Belle glanced at Ian in concern. "Do you think she's all right?" she whispered to him.

"Who knows?" he replied with a shrug. "She can definitely take care of herself under normal circumstances, but if she's been missing for several days..."

"I'm worried about her if Granny and Grayson are here. Did Granny tell you why they left her cottage?"

Shaking his head, Ian picked up the mirror. "Let's hope this works. Show me Daphne!" he commanded.

The silvery surface clouded over for a moment, then focused. It revealed Daphne in what appeared to be a wooden shed or barn of some sort, sitting on a dirt floor. She was filthy, and glaring at someone they couldn't see.

"This is a big mistake," she spat. "You'll see. Gustav is a bastard through and through, and won't keep his word to anyone, much less a woman."

"It won't matter," a female voice replied. "He's only good for a few things."

Belle gasped in shock. "Is that..." *Corinne? Or -*

"Felicity." Ian's voice was grim.

"I should have known," Belle muttered. "I'm so stupid. She told me that her name was Corinne, but there was something about her I just couldn't get over. She made me uncomfortable."

"What? You saw her? After she tried to drown you?" Ian grabbed her shoulders. "Belle, why didn't you tell me?"

"I had no idea that it was her," she retorted. "I met her walking into town just before Papa's workshop burned down. It never even occurred to me that she might be Felicity because I thought the curse kept her transformed into an object." Belle glared at Ian. "I had no idea that any of you could turn into humans, or maybe I would have wondered why she sounded so familiar at the time. We have to tell Ronan that Felicity and Gustav have Daphne!"

The balcony door flew open even as Belle rushed to it. Ronan stood there, outlined by the late afternoon light. "Show me," he demanded.

Ian held up the mirror. Daphne was still sitting on the ground, but she held a cup near her lips and some meat and bread sat on her lap.

"I promise you, this isn't going to work out like you've planned," she warned Felicity.

Felicity scoffed, but didn't say anything else. They heard the door open and close.

"Get me some paper," Belle ordered. "We don't know how long she'll be alone."

"Paper? What are you planning to do with that, princess, sketch her portrait?"

"Just shut up."

Ian gave her the paper and a pencil, and Belle quickly wrote a note, then handed it back to him. Holding his breath, Ian pushed it through the mirror's surface.

Ronan's jaw dropped.

They watched the paper fall into Daphne's lap. She just stared at it for a moment, then snatched it up. "It took you long enough," she scolded.

They all heard the little edge of tears in her voice.

"Where are you? Ronan is with us. G & G are safe," Daphne read in a whisper.

"I don't know, exactly. That fucking bastard Gustav was waiting for me on the way to Granny's cottage. I tried to run, but wolves chased me down. I'm afraid the mare didn't make it, and I probably wouldn't have either if Monique hadn't showed up. She swore to me that Ronan didn't know, and this wasn't supposed to happen."

A loud growl filled the room, coupled with popping noises. Ian pulled Belle away from Ronan, who dropped to all fours.

"Get ahold of yourself," Belle hissed. "We can't help her if you lose your temper."

He glared as he shook, trying to regain control.

"Monique said that she wasn't part of it either, but she overheard members of another pack talking about Grayson and Gustav one night. Something about trading Belle for Grayson, but that woman, Corinne, led them to me instead. So now Gustav wants to trade me for Belle."

"Can you hear the tavern or anything else? We need to find you," Belle wrote.

Daphne read it, then shook her head. "I'm in the woods. Probably not far from the falls, but I can't really tell. Monique put me on her back and ran, but Gustav shot her. She kept going as long as she could before I made her let me down and we parted ways. I think she survived, but I can't be sure. I cast a quick healing charm on her, then ran, trying to lead them away. I'm so sorry, Ronan."

"Tell her Monique survived. Her mate brought her back to the pack and she's recovering, but hasn't woken up yet. Wolves can sleep a long time to heal."

Belle nodded and wrote it down. Daphne sighed with relief when she got the note.

"Thank God. She did what she could, Ronan. Don't be angry with her. And don't let Belle come anywhere near here. Gustav has lost his mind. He keeps going on about Belle being the key to something, but he won't tell me what. Beast should probably stay away too, although I'd give my left leg to watch the two of you rip Gustav in half."

Daphne rubbed her chest as she spoke, glancing toward the door. "He desperately wants both of them, though, so you can't let them come, Ronan."

"Well, ripping him apart isn't going to happen since I can't exactly change back," Ian muttered. "Why would he want us?"

"You mean aside from having always wanted me, and you being a prince?" Belle retorted. "I can't think of any particular reason, what about you?"

"He doesn't want the prince. He wants the beast."

Belle shrugged and began writing. "The curse is broken and Beast turned into Ian. It's a long story, but Gustav won't be getting his head for a trophy."

Daphne read it. "Ian?! Seriously? I can't wait to hear how that happened. But still, I don't think it's about him wanting a trophy anymore. He said something about a witch wanting Beast, or Ian, or whoever he is. Something about trading him for his brother, if he won't come for me."

Ian stiffened beside her. "A witch? And what's Sam got to do with this?"

"Do you think it's the same bitch that cursed you here?" Ronan asked. "It would make sense if she knew the curse was broken. From what I understand, they can keep tabs on their most powerful spells."

"Probably," Ian said with a snort. "But I don't understand why. Sure, I'm a prince, but Evia is a small country, and not exactly a powerful one. There are much more profitable thrones to set one's sights on if she has this much power."

"That's not necessarily true, my dear," a new voice said from the doorway.

5

I an paled, then flushed with excitement. His fingers showed white around the knuckles where he gripped the mirror, and his hand tightened on Belle's arm.

Turning slowly, he was almost afraid to look up. "It's not possible..."

"Why not?" an older woman asked from the doorway. Belle stared at her, trying to place her voice.

She held her arms out. "Sebastian, Belle. I'm so happy to see you both." A very attractive older gentleman smiled at them from behind her.

"Maman! Papa, you're alive!" Ian nearly flew to them, dropping the mirror and dragging Belle along in his haste. "I thought she'd killed you when she turned you into statues!"

The stone lady. Of course. I assumed that she must still be alive when she came to my dreams, Belle thought as she hung back a little, not wanting to interrupt the family reunion.

The queen was having none of it. She grabbed Belle's hand from Ian's and pulled her in for a tight hug. "Thank you so much for everything you've done, Belle. I had all but given up hope before you came to the castle, and while I know it hasn't been easy, Sebastian loves you so very much. Thank you for giving him a chance," she whispered into Belle's ear.

"You've taught him so much that I feared he'd never learn, even before the curse. You've truly saved him, and all of us. If there's ever anything I can do for you, please don't hesitate to ask." She held Belle out at arm's length to look at her. "And please, call me Maman, or Clarisse."

Let me keep him, and don't make me go to court as a princess, or worse, queen, Belle silently replied. But aloud she just said, "I'm only glad I could help. I love him very much, too."

"Modest thing," the queen chided. "That's all right. I know how wonderful you are. And you, my boy, I'm so happy you've found each other."

She pulled Ian away from his father to hug him tightly as well. "I was afraid we'd never get out of those blasted statues, but you did it. I'm so proud of you."

"I had no idea you were even alive in there," Ian replied, pale-faced. "All this time, I thought you were dead because you couldn't move or talk. It didn't even occur to me that the statues were anything but crypts until Belle said that she could hear you in her dreams. I'm so sorry I couldn't do anything for you, and so sorry that damned enchantress came here because of me."

"Don't be silly, my boy. She didn't come just because of you. That may have been what she *said*, of course, but don't believe that nonsense. She and your father have been at each other's throats since before you were born."

"*What?!*" Ian and Belle demanded at the same time.

"Why didn't you ever warn me, or Sam, about her?"

"Is she going to come back?" Belle asked as well.

The queen looked to Ian's father, Samuel, for an answer.

"First, just let me say how lovely it is to meet you, Belle. I was thrilled when you first came into our little section of the garden, and I'm so happy that you've decided to stay. You're a very welcome addition to the family." Samuel bowed over her left hand.

"I see that my boy here has finally offered for you, so that will make me your father-in-law. Please, let me know if there's anything you ever need, and I can't wait to claim my dance with you at the wedding."

Dance with a king at my wedding? Belle felt her throat closing off and she groped for Ian's hand. "Erm, thank you, Your Highness."

"Please, Belle. It's just Pere, or Papa. Whichever you prefer."

"Th - thank you, Pere." The words were stilted coming out of her mouth and she blushed. Ian twined his fingers through hers and gave them a gentle squeeze.

"You were saying about the enchantress?" he prompted. The balcony door opened and closed behind them as Ronan went outside.

I want to go, too, Belle thought miserably. *There's not enough air in here.*

"Excuse me a moment," she murmured. "I need to speak with Ronan about my sister. She's been kidnapped and he's going after her."

"That's terrible," Clarisse exclaimed. "I'm so sorry, we had no idea!"

"It will be all right, I'm sure," Belle murmured. "We only just found out with the magic mirror. I'm sure Ronan wants to leave right away."

"Well, then what are we waiting for? Let's go rescue her!" Samuel volunteered.

"I'm afraid it's not that simple," Ian replied as Belle hurried toward the door. "The man who has Daphne is apparently in league with the enchantress, and has demanded that I come rescue her. We aren't sure if he knows that the curse is broken, but I'm assuming so. One of the kidnappers also used to be a maid here, but she ran away from the castle after trying to kill Belle."

"Tried to kill Belle?" Clarisse gasped. "In league with the enchantress?" She clutched onto Samuel's arm. "You have to do something about this! She was never supposed to go after our children, Samuel! That's against the law!"

Ian stared at her. "What law? I'm assuming you mean something other than the laws against attacking the royal family. How do you know her?"

Samuel nodded solemnly. "You'd better sit down for this, son. But first, bring Belle back in here and tell that Ronan fellow to wait. We need to figure out a good strategy before we go rushing in, and there's a lot that you need to know."

Belle and Ronan came back inside at Ian's request.

"How do you know the enchantress?" Ronan demanded. "Why would she get someone like Gustav involved with this?"

Samuel shrugged. "She's always been adept at finding tools and using them. As far as why Gustav in particular, I'm assuming that Belle could tell us more than I could about why he wants her."

They all looked at her in expectation.

"Honestly, I don't know. He's always seen me as a challenge, I suppose. Even when Papa and I first moved here, he took my lack of interest as a personal slight. Since then, he's constantly been trying to win me over. I'm sure that he'd move on to another girl if I ever just let him think I'm interested in him, but the idea of even pretending to enjoy his company makes me feel ill."

"I haven't met him myself, but my sister swears he's part ogre," Ronan added in. "And that sort are single-minded in their determination - once they've set their sights on something, they won't stop at anything to get it."

"An ogre, hmm? Then it makes sense that he won't let you go, now that he's fixated on you. That's one of the great downfalls of the species. Once they've become obsessed with something, it's literally impossible to leave it alone. Depending on how much of him is ogre, he wouldn't stop at just possessing you, my dear. It's more than likely that he would just keep tormenting you until he killed you. It wouldn't be the first time that's happened with a part-ogre, nor the first time that this bitch has encouraged it."

Belle shuddered and Ian put his arm around her. "Gustav will never get his hands on you, my love. I promise. Even if I have to kill him myself."

"But he has Daphne," Belle replied, shaken. *How would you protect me? Or my sister? Maybe my beast could, but Ian? Now that you're a human, I just don't see how. Maybe Ronan will be able to do something about it.* She flushed, embarrassed by her thoughts. *I should try to have a little more faith in Ian, he did knock Gustav onto his backside in town that day. But again, that was when Ian had Beast's strength.*

"So, how do you know the enchantress?" Ian pressed. "You said you two have a history."

Samuel glanced at Clarisse, who patted his knee. "Well. She's my sister."

"Your what?" Ian uttered. "You never told us that you had a sister."

"I was planning to tell you a lot when you were ready, but we didn't have as much time as I wanted. I'm not my real father's only child, or even his only son. Elavee, the bitch that did this to us, is my half-sister."

"Your *real* father?" Belle repeated. "So your mother…"

"She's long gone now, but yes. My mother married a mortal man while she was still the princess, and they ascended to the throne once my grandfather passed on. However, they had great difficulty getting with child, so my mother contacted a fairy that has occasionally helped our family. He spent one night with her, with her husband's consent, and a baby was born of the encounter."

"You." Ian said it matter-of-factly, like he wasn't completely baffled. "That fae is your real father. But the royal line came through your mother's side of the family, so it doesn't matter either way."

Samuel nodded. "My parents desperately wanted a family, and this seemed like the best way to get one. They didn't want to deal with the possibility of a human eventually letting the secret slip, or anyone finding out that I was conceived out of wedlock. The fairy in question wanted to guarantee that Evia would always be a haven for enchanted creatures, so it worked out well for both of them if the royal line was infused with a little fae blood."

"So your real father is still alive?" Belle asked quietly. Ian stilled beside her. "Ian told me that his grandparents were dead."

Samuel took a deep breath. "Yes. He's still alive. The fae are nearly immortal, which can translate oddly into human offspring. I age, and so far Ian and Sam both seem to, but some mixed children don't."

My children might stay young forever? Belle was taken aback by the thought. *How young? They might be eternally ten years old, or teenagers? Or even this age? What if Ian stops aging, too, at some point?* "Explain, please."

Samuel glanced at Clarisse again. She squeezed his hand. "Well, there's no way to tell how old they might be when they stop aging, if that's your question. It might be when someone is sixteen or sixty. And most don't even stop at all. The human portion of them seems to prevent that from happening ninety percent of the time."

"Don't worry, Belle," Clarisse tried to comfort her. "The more human blood is mixed with the fae, the less likely it becomes. The chances of Ian stopping without you are very slim, and the odds of your children doing so are even less."

"Even if he has an extended lifespan, we can ask my father to grant you one too. It wouldn't be a problem," Samuel assured her.

Ronan heaved an exasperated sigh and stood. The snug breeches strained at their seams. Clarisse raised an eyebrow as Belle blushed, looking away. "It's been an honor meeting you, Your Highnesses, but unless this fairy godfather is going to come help rescue Daphne, I think I'll leave you to the family reunion in peace. Gustav still has her and none of this talking is going to get her back."

"What are you going to do?" Belle asked in a worried tone. "If Elavee is a fairy enchantress, she might have a trap waiting."

"Can we see her with the mirror?" Ronan demanded. "Or Gustav? I thought it's supposed to be useful for this sort of thing."

Ian picked it up. "Show me Elavee." It swirled, but nothing came up.

"She's a full-blooded fairy," Samuel said. "I doubt human magic can track her."

"Show me Gustav," Ian demanded next. This time the mirror cleared to show Gustav pacing through the woods outside a small shed. Banked fires smoldered a little way away, and the doors to a nearby stable were thrown open. Several men milled about inside.

"Can we see that any better?" Ronan demanded, poking the woods beside the stable. "It looks familiar."

"I don't see anything except trees," Ian replied.

Ronan glared. "Just do it. I might know where they are."

Ian shook his head but asked the mirror for a better view regardless. The image moved, zooming in on the forest. A barren clearing with a stream cutting through the edge was nearby. Wolf tracks littered the scene.

"Damn it all to hell, I should have known," Ronan muttered. "That's at the edge of my pack's territory, on the other side of Granny's falls. It's about halfway between the cottage and your village, Belle."

A snarl curled his lips upward. "Wolves are involved in this, too. I need to gather my pack and put a stop to it."

"What do you mean, wolves are involved? Involved how?" Belle demanded. She grabbed Ronan's arm when he would have turned away. "That's my sister in there!"

"I know, and it's my -" he cut off, unwilling to continue.

"Your what?" she asked suspiciously. "What's going on between you and Daphne?"

"Nothing. Look, don't worry about it. She's not the pretty princess waiting for a knight in shining armor type, so get that out of your head. I'm not rushing in to rescue her because we're in love. We're friends, if even that. She's been protecting my son for months, which has now apparently caught up to her. To both of us."

"Protecting him from what?"

"A neighboring pack that would hurt him to get to me. They've been trying to take over for years, ever since Grayson was born and his mother died."

"Oh," Belle said slowly. "I'm so sorry." She turned to

Samuel. "Does Elavee have any weaknesses that you can tell us about, just in case she's there?"

He shook his head. "Nothing that I know of. I only met her once and she was irate that I even existed. My father had to order her from the grounds to get any peace. She's always said that mixing fae with humans should be forbidden."

"Fantastic," Ronan muttered, too low for anyone but Belle to hear. "Nevertheless, I'm going to get Daphne. Belle, Ian, Your Highnesses," he said with a bow. Belle was amazed that the breeches didn't rip as he bent.

"Have a lovely evening, and I'll bring Daphne back as soon as I can. I'm sure she'd love to meet you."

"Here. At least take something decent with you," Ian said. He stood and crossed to the armoire, taking out a pair of pants to throw at Ronan's back.

Ronan tossed them back as he stepped out onto the balcony. "No need." His voice was already changing, deepening and getting rougher as his face elongated into a muzzle. The skintight breeches ripped as he changed, shifting into a massive wolf.

He nodded once at them, then leapt over the balcony.

"Well. That was an interesting fellow," Clarisse murmured. "Do you know him well, Belle?"

"I just met him today, but I have the strangest feeling that he's going to be my brother-in-law," Belle replied. "He saved me from being eaten by his sister and her mate on the way here." *Was that really today? It feels like so long ago already.*

"What?!" Ian grabbed her arm. "Why didn't you tell me? Are you all right?"

"So much has happened since then. It's not that important, in the grand scheme of things. I doubt Monique really would have *eaten* us, but she seemed like she was about to. Ronan came in time anyway, so it doesn't matter."

"That's what you were talking about when you finally told me that you love me, isn't it? When you said you thought you were going to lose me?"

Belle nodded. Ian wrapped his arms around her in a tight hug. "I'm never letting you outside the gate again."

"Let's not get irrational," his mother interjected with a roll of her eyes. "I'm sure that Belle will take precautions so nothing like that will happen again. Plus Ronan is apparently in charge of the, ahem- werewolves, you said, and they can't hurt her without permission. Right, sweetheart?" She pinned Belle with a stare.

Hiding a smile, Belle nodded. "Of course. Nothing really happened, anyway. It's just something that Ronan has to work out with his sister. She's clearly seen the error of her ways if she tried to help Daphne get away from Gustav."

"I still don't like it."

"Now, son. You can't keep her here against her will forever." Samuel clapped him on the shoulder. "I understand it's scary to love someone, but there will be no more prisoners."

"Like he could even if he tried," Belle huffed as she poked his side. "He's already found out that he doesn't get to tell me what to do."

"I knew you'd be good for him," Clarisse said, beaming. "Now, then. It's been over a decade since we've seen Sam, and I think going to visit is a fantastic idea. His father needs to speak with him about this Elavee nonsense anyway. I'm honestly shocked that the curse was allowed to happen at all."

She turned and narrowed her eyes in anger at her husband. "You told me that she could never hurt them. You promised when we got married."

"There will be consequences, I'm sure," Samuel assured her. "We'll figure out why she was able to do what she did, and why no one came to break the curse earlier. My brother and father must have known something, and I plan to get to the bottom of it."

"I think you should go to Sedonia as soon as possible," Ian interrupted. "Regardless of why or how Elavee got to us, the fact is that she did. She may have been leaving Sam alone all this time because she had us where she wanted us, but now that the curse is broken she might go after him. I think it would be safer for all of you there."

His parents stared at him. "But what about you, and Belle? We only just woke up."

"I know. You don't have to decide now, but I want you to think about it. We'll be fine here, but with this Gustav-the-ogre fellow and werewolves in league with Elavee, I think it would be better if you had more protection. You said she's always been after you, so it stands to reason she'll try something else."

Samuel nodded slowly, even as Clarisse shook her head. He squeezed her hand.

"Ian's right," Samuel told her. "It makes sense that she'll try again, now that the curse is broken. We need to prepare for that, and at least speak with Rumsfeld. I can almost guarantee you that he is the one who took over Sam's training and raised him."

Clarisse frowned, but eventually sighed her agreement. "We'll talk about it."

They stayed a few more minutes, then decided to retire to their rooms.

"We have a lot to talk about, and we know you two would like some time alone. We'll see you in the morning." Clarisse gave them both firm hugs but her arms lingered around Ian. "I'm so happy to be able to be with you again, my boy," she said with a sniffle. "So many times I wished I could comfort you and tell you it would be all right, but that damned statue wouldn't move. I can't tell you how thrilled I was when Belle came and stayed."

"Me, too, Maman. Me, too."

6

Ian took her hand as his parents left the room. "Are you alright?"

I seriously doubt it. "I don't know. That was a lot to take in. Not only does it sound like your father expects you to be king soon, but you're also part fae so any children we have will be, too. Even though technically *he* should be sitting on the throne of Evia, but no one has brought that up, and everyone in the kingdom probably thinks he's dead anyway. So you and Sam have to work out who is going to be in charge. It would be easier to just make Sam keep the title and not worry about it, but I think that you should at least check with him first."

"Even though you don't want anything to do with it?"

Belle winced a little. "The very notion of going to court terrifies me. I think being queen would give me a heart attack, and I'm sure it will get interesting from time to time when I meet more of your previous conquests."

He blushed. "I'm sorry. I was young, and never even thought about how it would affect my future. Our future." He pressed a kiss against her palm. She thought of the times that Beast had done that same action and had to suppress a shiver. "You'd make a wonderful queen, by the way. Evia would be lucky to have you."

Waving away his apology and ignoring the rest of his words, Belle allowed him to pull her onto his lap on the edge of the bed. "I know. It doesn't matter now because it was all in the past, but that doesn't mean I have to look forward to the potentially awkward balls and soirees, now does it?"

"What if I promise to make it up to you after each one?" His eyes glinted with mischief as he ran a hand up the outside of her thigh. "I'm sure we can figure something out to make it a little more bearable."

"Just as long as no one else tries to kill me over it."

Ian's hand tightened on her leg. "No one else will hurt you, or take you away from me. I promise. What did Felicity say when you saw her in town?"

"It was a very odd conversation, but it makes more sense now that I know who she really was. She started off trying to make me jealous by telling me that she'd been intimate with Ian, my merchant friend. She got very confused when I didn't care. I guess she thought I knew who you were in human form, but I had no idea so her plan to upset me backfired. Then she told me that I'm too beautiful not to use it to my advantage, whatever that meant. I can only guess that she meant I was using my face to gain favor with you because you're the prince, since that's what she tried to do by sleeping with you before the curse. But being prettier than everyone else has never really worked out well for me, and she seemed surprised when I told her that. She was also a little shocked to hear that Gustav is quite forceful with women, even when they don't return his affections. I don't think she expected me to try to warn her."

"You don't care that we slept together?"

Belle rolled her eyes. "Of course that's the only part you listened to. It didn't matter because I had no idea that you were my Beast, you idiot. Of course I care now. But Ian the merchant had no claim on my heart, so why would his exploits have been important?" Her lips pursed at the end of the question.

"I guess you're right." He paused for a moment, thinking. "Do you think you can feel the same about me now that I'm Ian again? Instead of the beast that you fell in love with?"

She grabbed his collar and pulled him down so that they were eye to eye. *Even those have changed a little,* she thought with an internal sigh. *I hope nothing in his heart has.* "I fell in love with who you were on the inside," Belle declared. "As long as you're the same in here," she poked his chest, "then what you look like doesn't matter. It will take some getting used to, but I'm certain everything will be fine."

"I know how much you loved that body. Its strength, warmth and occasionally the horns," he teased. "Do you think you can be satisfied with my human version?"

"I'm sure everything will be fine," she repeated. She didn't sound quite as confident this time and he raised an eyebrow.

"I'm going to miss certain things about the beast, it's true." The whispered confession made Ian's heart twist. "But not what you think. Yes, your horns were fantastic, and your mouth even more so, but that's not all, you lecher."

She rubbed her cheek against his, then settled it on his shoulder. Ian gathered her close and leaned back on the bed, gently stroking her back.

"I think I'm going to miss your expressions the most. It took me a little while, but I always knew what you were thinking by the way your ears would flick, your lips would curl or how your tail would rest or writhe, depending on your mood. I'm going to have to relearn all of that now, and I'm not very good with people as a general rule. It's a little intimidating."

"My brave Belle, ready to face down a monster, but afraid of getting to know a human? That doesn't make much sense."

"No, it doesn't. But it's still who I am."

"And it makes you perfect." He hugged her. "I know it's a big adjustment. Everything that you were used to about your lover's body suddenly changed, and became someone you never thought you'd be intimate with. It makes sense if it's a little awkward at first, but I'll do my best to make it easier on you."

Ian rolled them over, flipping her onto her back and cuddling against her side. She stiffened for a moment as he brushed his fingertips across her collarbone, then down her arm like Beast used to do. Goosebumps followed in the wake of his touch. "I don't think I'm ready for anything like this yet -" Her heart protested even as her lips uttered the words. *Even though I really want to. But what does that say about me, ready to let him deceive me, then fall right into bed? Although I suppose he had good reason, what with not wanting to make the curse completely permanent. And he was never pushy as Ian, like Gustav was.*

"I know, I know. But I loved lying with you like this before, and I want to try it out as a man." He lowered his head to her chest and nuzzled his cheek against her softness. "Remember how we would just lie here and talk? You would stroke my mane and I would tell you stories about growing up in the capital. It was so relaxing."

Yes, but we were usually naked, so you'd end up kissing your way across my skin while you talked. And your fur would barely tickle, leaving behind the most delicious sensations while you moved. Her face heated up as he reminded her just how much she'd enjoyed his previous form. She hoped he didn't notice. "Lying with you like this was nice, yes." *More than nice.*

Heat began to pool in her belly as Ian ran his fingertips over the crook of her elbow, then back up her arm. They almost brushed the outer curve of her breast and her breath hitched the slightest bit.

Please tell me he didn't hear that, she silently begged. *I'm not sure I'm ready for this with Ian.* A mischievous little voice, the one that had delighted in pointing out all of the most promising bits of Madame Fontaine's book, asked, *Why not? You wouldn't think twice if he was still the beast. Being human might even make it better. You already know you love him, and you're getting married, for goodness' sake. Why not relax and enjoy it?*

The temptation pulled at her, sending her thoughts careening back to all of those stolen moments that had started out just like this. The hours of pleasure they'd had in this bed, talking or kissing, clothed or naked, came rushing back all at once.

"Are you thinking about Daphne?"

"Um, yes." *Not at all,* Belle thought with a cold shot of guilt. "I wonder how she's faring, and what Gustav plans to do with her."

"Knowing Daphne, she's probably just fine. She might even have Gustav begging for mercy by this point, with a pig's tail sprouted from his forehead."

Belle laughed at the mental image.

"We can check on her again if you'd like," Ian offered. He leaned over and grabbed the mirror's handle when she nodded. Its surface swirled, then revealed Daphne curled up on the floor in a corner, her eyes closed. The even rise and fall of her chest reassured them both.

"See, she's just taking a nap. It'll be a few hours at best before Ronan and his pack can get to her if she's near the village." Ian put the mirror back down. "I'm sure they'll find her and bring her home by this time tomorrow."

"Home here?"

"I'm assuming so. I doubt it would be safe for her to stay at Granny's any more. In fact they should all just stay here, Grayson too."

Belle smiled as relief washed through her, dispelling the last of her tension. Ian propped himself up on one elbow and peered down at her. "Why do you look so relieved? You didn't honestly think I'd make them stay out in the woods, did you?"

"No, of course not! It's just... I wasn't sure what to expect. I wasn't even sure if we're staying here."

"What do you mean? Where else would we go?" His brows scrunched together as he looked down at her. "Do you want to leave?"

"No, I just thought that since you're human now, you'd want to go to the capital with your parents and Sam." She glanced down at her fingers, which seemed to be picking a thread out of her sleeve of their own accord. She stilled them and dropped the thread, daring to run them along his side, instead. "I don't want you to feel obligated to stay."

"We aren't obligated to do anything, Belle. Not anymore. This is our home and as long as you're happy here, I'm happy. I know you want to see the world, and we can make that happen, too. Just tell me what you want and I'll take care of it."

Ian stroked her cheek with the back of his fingers, smoothing away the stress. "I just want to be wherever you are. If you want to stay and having your sister here makes you feel better, then let's ask her and Granny Rousseau to move in. Your papa is already, so she may as well, too."

"Thank you for that, by the way," Belle said as she finally met his eyes. "I know that was difficult for you, especially since the curse was still in place. But I appreciate it."

"My beauty. You really don't know, do you?" He leaned down to press a soft kiss against the corner of her lips. "I would have done anything to get you back. You're everything to me, and I was an idiot not to see it sooner. I'm so very sorry that I didn't value you enough, and drove you away in the first place. You could have brought the entire town back with you and I would have welcomed them with open arms, if only it meant that you were here to stay."

He's still my sweet Beast. I'll always stay. "You might regret that, now that you've agreed to marry me. That's forever, you know," she teased. The edge of her lips tingled where he'd kissed her. She rubbed them together.

"Mmm, it had better be." Ian's chest vibrated against hers as he made a low noise of approval. Belle couldn't hold back a shudder as he trailed his fingers down her arm, then twined them through hers. He pulled her hand up beside her head and pressed it into the mattress.

Bending down, he kissed her cheek once more, his lips lingering on her skin. Belle inhaled sharply and clenched his fingers.

He made that noise again, so much like Beast's growl, and rubbed his cheek against hers. Belle turned into it, rubbing back.

He's my fiancé, and like I told him earlier, the time for modesty has long since passed, she reassured herself. *I want this, so there's no reason not to enjoy myself. No reason not to enjoy him. But now there's also no reason to stop.* The last thought renewed her nervousness, but for totally new reasons. *What if it isn't the same? Or hurts too much, now that he'll finally fit inside me? What if... what if I don't know what to do and I disappoint him?*

Their lips met. Belle relaxed under the kiss, letting it wash through her. Ian nipped and teased at her until she opened for him and thrust her tongue against his, unable to take it anymore. Releasing her hand, he slid his palm to her back, pulling her onto her side. Against him, while still giving her plenty of room to push away if she wanted.

A brief flash of gratitude registered as Belle skimmed her hand over his chest. The muscles clenched under her touch and she smiled. *He's not pressuring me, just enjoying as usual. There's no need to be worried, even though he looks so different. He's still my Beast.*

Growing bolder, she swept her hand down his front to the hem of his shirt. Ian pulled her closer, his kiss growing a little desperate as she played with the edge.

"Please." His voice was ragged. "I've waited so long to feel your hands on my skin."

7

H is response tore at her heart, and she couldn't do anything but oblige. Ian shuddered as she slid her hand under the linen, trailing her fingertips across his side.

It was hot, yet silky beneath her touch. Lost in the texture, Belle pressed against him and went higher, lifting the edge of his shirt as she did.

He sucked on her bottom lip, pulling it between his teeth as he drove his hand into her hair. She moaned and curled her fingers against his back, lightly scraping him with her nails. Suddenly overwhelmed with the need to see and feel all of him, she jerked on the shirt, struggling to get it up past his shoulders.

Pulling his lips from hers, Ian trailed kisses along her jaw. "Tell me what you want," he whispered into her ear. He licked the sensitive spot beneath her lobe, then lightly bit her throat.

Belle bucked against him. Her breasts ached and little jolts of electricity seemed to radiate out from her nipples every time they pressed against his chest.

"Take this off," she demanded. "I want to see you." He kissed her collarbone as he moved his hand, palming her hip. Her skirt bunched beneath his fingers as he went lower, dragging it up out of his way.

"And then what?" he breathed. Belle's leg tingled where he grabbed it, pulling her knee over his side. His erection pressed against her, and she had to fight the urge to grind against it.

The edge of her skirt was finally within his grasp. Belle arched against him as he grabbed it, his fingers meeting her bare skin as well. They left burning trails of heat as he made his way up the back of her thigh.

Belle moaned. He stopped when his fingers were mere inches from her center, setting her on fire, but refusing to go any farther.

"Beast..." she pleaded. He caressed a little higher and she writhed against him, willing him to just touch her.

Ian groaned as his fingers met the crease where her leg ended and her lips began. Slick desire coated them.

"Christ, Belle. Tell me now if you still want to stop. You're dripping wet and I'm not going to be able to resist if we do anything else." He stroked back and forth, teasing the edge of her pussy.

Belle arched her back in response, rubbing against his hand as she pulled him down for another kiss.

Ian's middle finger dipped inside her, raking down her slit. He hissed as she clenched around him.

"I don't want to stop," she whispered. "I want you. I want this."

He groaned, deep in his chest. "I love you so much. You're more than I could ever deserve."

She tried to protest and he kissed her again, silencing her words. Molten fire swept through her as he teased her with both his mouth and his fingers, stroking between her lips. Belle arched, begging for more.

He gave it to her.

His thumb swept forward, rubbing around her clit while he slid his first finger into her slick channel.

Belle broke the kiss with a gasp. Squeezing her eyes shut, she bit her lip as the new sensations rolled through her. Ian feathered kisses down her throat, then closed down on the curve of her shoulder.

Her channel tightened again, squeezing his finger. He groaned aloud as she gasped, pulling his hair.

Pleasure spiraled within her as he moved his hand, sliding out, then back in again. He pressed forward while he rubbed her clit, hitting a spot deep inside that he never had as Beast.

"That feels amazing," she moaned. "Don't stop."

"Never," he promised, pulling back to watch her face. Her eyelids squeezed shut as he added a second finger, stretching her untried flesh. "I have to taste you."

Her eyes popped back open as he pushed her onto her back and scooted down her body. There was a brief sensation of loss, emptiness as he removed his hand to shove her skirt and petticoat out of the way, but Belle hardly had time to notice.

Ian raked his nails down the inside of her thighs, making her shiver as he dove in for a kiss. Licking and sucking on her clit while his fingers pressed back inside her, he had her on the verge of climax within seconds.

"Oh!" She nearly came off of the bed as her belly clenched, riding out the delicious sensations radiating up from her sex. "Beast!"

He growled, rubbing his tongue across her even faster.

Her hands found his hair again and pulled, desperate for more.

Ian sucked, hard, flicking across her clit. It was all she needed to shatter around him.

Screaming his name, Belle arched against the mattress, riding his hand and mouth. He kept going, sucking and tasting her until she let go of his hair, gasping for breath.

Ian pressed his forehead against her belly, breathing sweet, greedy gulps of her scent. His cock felt like it was on the verge of bursting inside his too-large pants.

"Come here," Belle beckoned as she pulled on his shirt again. "Take this off. I want to see all of you."

He didn't move for a moment, afraid that the slightest friction would bring him to orgasm. Finally he lifted her hips back to his mouth and gave her one more long lick, sliding his tongue deep into her folds.

"Mmm, that feels amazing. But I want you now, not just your mouth. I think we've waited long enough."

Ian nipped her inner thigh, making her jump before getting up onto his knees. Her legs were splayed out on either side of him and he grabbed her ass, pulling her bottom half into his lap. Unable to resist, he rubbed her pussy along his length, staring down at her bare skin meeting his pants.

There were too many clothes between them still.

"Take them off," Belle murmured. "And that damn shirt, or I think I might scream."

Ian laughed, then set her back down on the bed. Whipping his shirt over his head, he tossed it to the floor and absently ran a hand down his bare chest. Everything still felt so new.

"Now your dress," he said said with a growl. "I can't believe it's stayed on this long."

Belle didn't move. Eyes wide, she just stared at him.

His body was amazing. Years of running and using the beast's massive strength had left Ian covered in thick muscles. His wide shoulders flexed as he shifted above her, moving onto his hands and knees. Belle couldn't resist reaching up to trace his lines, starting at his bulging pectorals and ending with his shadowed abdomen.

Her mouth watered at the idea of biting each muscle, as she had before.

"Enjoying yourself?" he asked in a raspy voice laced with amusement.

Belle blushed as her eyes snapped back up to his. She grinned and raked her nails over the vee at his hips. His eyes nearly rolled back in his head as he thrust against her, grinding their sexes together.

"Maybe. Why don't you get these pants off and find out for yourself?" she teased.

"Not going to be able to hold back if I'm naked -" he stopped with a groan as Belle leaned up and bit one of his pecs.

"Fuck, Belle. I don't want to be rough for your first time, but I don't know if I'll be able to help it if you keep that up."

He nearly panted as she did it again, this time closer to his nipple. She kissed the spot afterward, soothing his skin with her tongue. He rotated his hips against hers, grinding against her clit.

Belle let out a moan as the pressure began to build again, causing another wet gush to seep through his pants. She fell back against the bed even as her fingers plucked on his nipples, tugging with just enough pressure.

He groaned as he shifted his weight onto one arm, using the other hand to jerk on the front laces of her dress. Soon it gaped open enough for him to slide his hand inside and cup one of her breasts.

Belle arched as he lightly pinched its peak, drawing the stiff nub to attention. Scooting back down, Ian nuzzled against her cleavage before pulling the dress apart and diving in. Kissing, licking and sucking his way across the bottom of one breast, he made Belle writhe in tortured pleasure before finally drawing her nipple into his mouth.

"Your pants. Now," she demanded. The broad expanse of his back called to her and she ran her hands across it.

Ian's shoulders clenched beneath her caress, so she did it again. He kept unlacing her dress as he flicked his tongue back and forth over her hard nipple, making her moan. Ian alternated between sips and deep sucks, keeping her on edge as he built her back up towards another climax.

Belle shifted beneath him, raking her nails lightly across his back. He retaliated by closing his teeth around her nipple, just firmly enough to make her arch but not enough to hurt. Releasing it from his mouth, he sat back up on his knees, forcing her along with him.

"Lift your arms," he ordered before whisking the dress and petticoat up over her head. Finally naked, Belle wrapped herself around him, pressing their bodies together. Ian hugged her back, reveling in the sensation of her skin against his.

Belle gently pressed her lips against his, some of their frantic passion abandoned for the moment.

He gave a satisfied purr of happiness, despite his aching cock. "I used to dream about holding you like this," he murmured against her lips. "I never thought it would be possible, but I used to dream about it."

"Me too," she admitted quietly.

Ian raised an eyebrow. "You thought of me? Ian?"

Belle rubbed her cheek against his, then laid her head on his shoulder. "Not Ian, necessarily. But you as a man, holding me without worrying about hurting me. Being happy."

He rubbed her back, tracing her curves. "I've always been happy with you." His thumb brushed against the side of her breast, making her jump.

She tightened her legs around his waist as she kissed his shoulder. "I know. But you were always holding back, too. Now you don't have to anymore."

His eyes took on that orangey glow she loved so much. He gave her a half-wild smile as he cupped her breast, squeezing it.

"I know."

He lifted her against him as he lowered them both to the bed, keeping his mouth in line with her chest. He sucked her nipple back into his mouth as he stroked down her belly with one hand, then brushed his knuckles over her sex before popping the buttons open on his pants.

The baggy clothes nearly fell off on their own, leaving him free. Belle gasped as his hot length lay against her legs.

"I want to see you. Touch you like you did me."

Ian shook his head with a reluctant smile. "Next time, my beauty. I'm not going to last if you try it now, and I promise, you'll have plenty of opportunities."

Belle lifted an eyebrow. Before Ian could react, she sat up, forcing him to the side while she ran her hand along his thick cock.

"No holding back, remember?" she whispered in his ear. Her fingers closed around him and she gave him a languid stroke while she kissed his ear.

He clenched his teeth together, desperately trying to keep from cumming. "Fuck, Belle. That feels so good."

"You know what would feel even better?" she asked quietly, rubbing her cheek against his again. He closed his eyes and dropped his forehead to her shoulder.

"What?" His voice was ragged as she kept stroking him.

"My tongue, licking just here." She swiped her thumb over his head, spreading the drop of precum there to the ridge of his head.

Ian groaned as his cock jerked in her hand. "Belle, I can't-"

"Can't what?" she teased. "Can't wait to be inside me? Because I can't either. See?"

She dropped her knees to either side and slid her other hand down to her sex. "I'm so ready for you."

He stared while she pulled her glistening lips open and rubbed her middle finger over her clit.

He didn't move, so still she wondered if he was breathing. Tendrils of nervousness wound their way into her mind. *Why isn't he doing anything? He liked it when I touched myself before.*

She stopped and released his shaft. Moving her hand away, Belle let out a shaky breath. *Maybe I shouldn't have pushed him -*

Ian crashed into her, shoving her back onto the bed. His lips crushed hers in a fevered kiss, devouring her as though he were starving. Belle wrapped her arms around his shoulders and clung to him while he drove his fingers into her waiting center.

She gasped, lifting her hips against his hand. The pace he set was hard and fast, his fingers twisting and pressing inside her until she couldn't take it anymore.

"Please, Beast, more! I need -"

He bit her shoulder, hard, as he pressed down on her

clit. His hooked fingers pulled upward inside her, nearly lifting her off the bed.

"Oh, fuck!" Belle cried out the unfamiliar word as she came again, orgasm breaking through her in waves. She hadn't stopped reeling, clenching around his hand when suddenly it was gone and Ian's hips were against hers instead.

Dazed, she lifted her head to watch as he thrust slowly against her, dragging the underside of his cock along her wet slit. His chest vibrated as he growled, his whole body tense.

"I wanted to go slow for your first time," he managed from behind clenched teeth, "but I don't think I can anymore. You're just so..."

He stopped talking as he grabbed himself and rubbed his head across her entrance. Belle's breath caught as he barely slipped inside her body.

He leaned his head down and kissed her, claiming her mouth as he sank into her pussy. Belle's eyes widened at the invasion, but she couldn't keep herself from pressing against him when he would have stopped, taking him deeper.

She felt a little pinch of pain, a mere fluttering of discomfort compared to the pleasure, before he was sheathed entirely within her. White heat radiated outward from her sex, burning as she stretched around him.

She loved it.

"Are you all right?" Ian asked in concern when she didn't move or say anything. She met his gaze and smiled, then hooked her legs around his hips.

"Does it hurt anymore?" he pressed.

Belle shook her head.

"Good." Ian pulled back and gave her a quick, hard thrust, burying himself inside her sweetness. She gasped in surprised delight, then moaned as he did it again. Ian kept going, driving his cock deep every time.

"Fuck, Belle, you're so tight. I'm not going to be able to keep this up much longer."

She was still lost in the experience, making little noises of pleasure every time he sank into her. Swearing, he adjusted the angle of their hips so that he rubbed against her clit with every thrust.

White-hot pleasure flooded her senses, pushing her over the edge. Belle pressed her head back against the pillows and raked her nails down his shoulders as she came. Overwhelmed as she tightened around him, Ian couldn't hold back anymore and joined her in climax.

8

T he afternoon was waning before they finally got out of bed to check the mirror. It looked as though Ronan and his pack were on their way to rescue Daphne, who was still locked in the shed, fast asleep.

Belle passed her as vague of a note as she dared, hoping that Felicity or Gustav didn't find it before Daphne woke. Ian finally took the mirror from her and promised they'd check again after getting cleaned up and eating.

Their stomachs growling, they shared a languid bath before getting dressed and heading toward the kitchen. Belle held the mirror in one hand, and Ian's in the other. It reminded her of the first time they'd been intimate, when she was walking down the same hallway with him as the beast.

"I hope no one is upset that you haven't seen them before now," Belle murmured. "I'm sure Etienne and Mrs. Ambly have been dying to talk to you."

"I think you're the one they want to see," Ian replied. "They all know me. Maybe even too well, after being locked up in here for years."

"Still," Belle murmured. "We probably should have spent time with them first, like you asked."

Wrapping his arm around her shoulders, Ian nuzzled her hair. "Not a chance. I probably would have killed anyone that came through our door after my parents left."

Laughing softly, she cuddled into his side. "Well, here we go."

The kitchen was surprisingly empty, aside from a tall, robust man standing beside the stove.

"Cookie?" Belle called out, a little nervous. "Is that you?"

The man turned with a smile. "Belle! It's lovely to finally meet you in person, as it were." He held his arms out and she hurried over for a hug.

"I always knew you would be the one," Cookie declared. "The master here almost messed it up, but I think knowing he'd have to eat nothing but pea soup convinced him to straighten up, eh, Master?"

Ian harrumphed, but couldn't hide a smile when he heard Belle giggle.

"I'm sure that was it, Cookie. No one could live on pea soup alone, especially when the rest of your cooking is so delicious."

He preened under the compliments. "Exactly. The king and queen are in the dining room right now, and Madame Rousseau just joined them. I made plenty of roast pheasant, so if you need anything else, my stove is at your command."

He gave her a low, sweeping bow and kissed the back of her hand. Belle laughed at his flamboyance, which earned a tight smile from Ian.

He set his hand at the small of her back, urging her toward the dining room doors. "Are you usually in the habit of hugging strange men?" he half-teased.

"Why, Beast, are you jealous?" Belle wrapped her arm

around his waist and poked his opposite ribs. "You know you're the only man, or monster, for me. I'm excited that they've all changed back and Cookie looked so happy. It would have been rude not to be friendly, especially since he's taken such wonderful care of us. I couldn't do his job and I'm happy he's here."

"I suppose you're right," Ian groused as he hooked one arm around her shoulders. "It will just take some getting used to."

"I'm sure you'll live." She patted the back of his hand, earning a quick glance from the corner of his eye. She countered it with an over-bright smile and he finally relaxed.

He's so jealous. He's definitely going to have to get over that, especially considering that I'm the one who will always be stuck wondering if women I meet have seen him naked. I suppose then they'll be the ones jealous of me for getting to keep him. Her brief flash of annoyance at the thought faded into smug delight, surprising her. *None of them matter now, and he'll have to realize that no one else matters to me either.*

"What are you thinking?" he whispered as they walked into the dining room. Granny Rousseau and a young boy sat at one end of the table, and Ian's parents were at the other.

"Just that I love you, and all of the ladies you've been with before me are going to be jealous that I get to keep you all to myself," she replied with a wink. "They won't even know what they missed out on when you were Beast. I'm the only one to ever know, just like you're the only one to know me. So really, we're even on that count."

Ian stared at her, opened his mouth to reply, then shut it again. Samuel stood at the end of the table and called out a welcome.

"Sebastian, Belle. Come sit with us a moment. We're going to retire soon, but Cook has prepared a lovely dinner."

Granny Rousseau and the little boy looked up as well.

"We'll be there in a moment," Ian replied. His father sat back down.

"Aunt Belle?" Grayson's high-pitched baby voice tugged at her heart and she knelt, holding her arms out to him.

He scooted off of his chair and ran. Throwing himself into her arms, he nearly knocked her over, but Ian lent a supporting hand as she stood. The child clung to her, refusing to let go.

"You must be Grayson," she murmured. "I'm so happy to see you again."

He buried his little face against her neck.

"He's been asking for you since we got here," Granny said as she came up beside them. "He remembers that you saved him from Gustav, and that you're Daphne's sister."

"Where is she?" Grayson asked without looking up. "Will she be home soon?"

Belle rubbed his back as she swayed from side to side with him. "I hope so, baby. Your daddy went to get her."

Grayson sniffled and relaxed, but didn't let go of her.

"It's nearly his bedtime," Granny explained. "He sleeps more than the average child."

"Did you eat all of your dinner?" Belle asked gently. "You need a full belly to sleep well."

He shook his head.

"Do you think we could bring his plate over and sit with your parents?" Belle asked. "I don't want to put him down if he wants me, but he needs to eat."

"I'm sure it will be fine," Ian replied after a moment. Seeing Belle with the little dark-haired boy in her arms was making it unexplainably hard to talk. *I can give her children now. I knew she wanted them before, but we can actually have our own, now that I'm human again.* The thought shook him.

She may be pregnant already, for all I know. I didn't even think about using protection.

"What's wrong?" she asked. "You look like you've seen a ghost."

I hope she is. "Nothing. I was just thinking. Of course we can bring his plate down. Granny, would you like to join us as well?"

Granny Rousseau cast an uncertain glance at the king and queen's end. They were leaning together, chatting with their heads close.

"Are you sure?"

Ian offered her his arm. "Definitely. I would like them to meet you regardless. They should know who saved Sam and helped the rest of us. You gave me, and everyone else under the curse, a way to keep our humanity."

"Except them," Granny replied nervously. "My counter-curse never worked on their statues, and I'm not sure why. You would have known that they were still alive in there a long time ago if it had."

"No one is going to blame you for that," Ian comforted her. "What help you were able to give was a blessing and wholly unexpected. Please, come meet them."

Granny glanced at Belle, who nodded her head over Grayson's shoulder. The boy was still hanging onto her like he wasn't going to let go any time soon.

"Will you grab Grayson's and Granny's plates, my love?" Belle asked, effectively settling the matter. Ian did and Granny trailed after them to his parents' end of the table, still a little apprehensive.

"Maman, Pere, this is Granny Rousseau and Grayson," Ian introduced. Granny gave a stiff curtsy and Grayson just pressed even tighter against Belle. To everyone's surprise, the king stood and offered Granny Rousseau a low bow.

"Thank you for the help that you gave both of my sons, and all of the other inhabitants of this castle, in their hour of greatest need," he said. "If there is ever anything that the crown can do for you, please don't hesitate to ask."

Granny blushed. "Oh, it was nothing, Your Grace. I did what anyone would do when Sam made his way to my neck of the woods. He was just a little boy, after all."

"Not just anyone. You took in a traumatized child, believed his unbelievable story about the curse, and went above and beyond after that by escorting him back to the capital. You made sure he was safe from both Elavee and those who would have taken advantage of him by giving him to the advisors, and keeping the whole thing quiet. Then you came back and faced the beast to help here where you could. I know it wasn't nothing, Madame Rousseau."

She blushed and stuttered.

"Our bodies may have been sealed inside the statues, but we never stopped watching over our children, Granny. I'm sure you understand," Queen Clarisse added. "It looks like you do a fair bit of watching out for children yourself."

She smiled gently at Grayson, who sat on Belle's lap. He turned away from her and the bite of meat that Belle was trying to coax into his mouth. Cuddling in again, he gave a sudden shudder and changed, transforming from an adorable little boy into an equally adorable little wolf cub.

Belle dropped the bit of pheasant in surprise. Cub-Grayson's tail thumped as he snapped it up from her lap, then closed his eyes, let out a contented huff and went to sleep.

"Well. I suppose that's one way of telling us he doesn't want to talk," Belle murmured as she stroked his little back.

Granny nodded, then glanced back at the king and queen. "I apologize, Your Highnesses, he doesn't realize who you are. He's had a very trying time of it over the last few months."

"It's fine," Clarisse reassured her. "I understand. Children take a bit to warm up to people, and that's perfectly acceptable. We are strangers, after all. Now please, sit and eat."

Servants had loaded their plates with a bit of everything on the table, so Ian and Belle dug right in.

"Have you thought about when you're going to the capital to see Sam? Or how you're going to explain everything to him?" Ian asked after a drink of wine.

"As soon as possible. I think it's too dangerous to stay here since Elavee is trying to stir up trouble again. We should all go to the capital together. Tomorrow, if we can," Samuel decreed.

He held up a hand as Belle began to protest.

"I understand that your sister is in danger, and you want to wait here for her rescue, but you and Sebastian need to come to Sedonia as well."

Belle looked at Ian, who nodded after a moment. "We'll talk about it. I can't promise anything until we see how all of this works out with Daphne and we discuss what Belle wants to do, but we'll talk about it." He reached over and gave her hand a squeeze. "She wants to see the world, so we might not stay with you and Sam long."

Queen Clarisse's face clouded over. "But -"

"I know. I should be King, instead of Sam. Actually," Ian glanced at his father, "Pere' should still have the title. We want to spend time with you, of course, but I think that after all of this it would be nice to just have some time as a normal couple. Without all of the stress and pressure of court, or anything like that. Just give Belle and I time to adjust to my new body, and our relationship. We did just get engaged."

"Are you thinking of eloping?" Granny Rousseau asked shrewdly.

Both the King and Queen stared at her in shock, then turned sharp gazes on Belle and Ian.

9

‒‒‒‒‒‒

"**Y**ou can't -"

"A royal wedding is absolutely necessary -"

Belle hugged Grayson, who stirred as their voices rose. Forcing herself to relax, she simply said, "We haven't had enough time to even begin to think about it all. I'm sorry, but I'm not sure I want a huge wedding with hundreds of guests. We weren't even sure where our relationship stood yesterday, and today we're talking about a royal wedding with Ian, instead of a little ceremony here with Beast. It's all just so -" she stopped for a moment, overwhelmed as her heart pounded. She bent, rubbing her face in the cub's fur as she just concentrated on breathing for a moment.

"I'm not saying no, but can we please have some time before anyone starts planning anything? I haven't even thought of eloping, or anything like that. Whatever we do though, I promise that we'll invite you both and my Papa," Belle assured them. "Even if you're the only guests, I wouldn't dream of having it without you."

But eloping sounds so wonderful right now, she thought.

Why did Granny have to mention it? Ian reached under the table and squeezed her knee, as though he knew what she was thinking.

"We clearly can't have a formal wedding right away," he agreed. "There is the one little matter of everyone thinking that I'm dead. Honestly, I don't see why any of the court should know otherwise, aside from Sam. I'd hate to throw the country into a turmoil by changing monarchs after so many years, not to mention whatever Sam thinks of it. Hell, he might even like being the king."

No one said anything for a moment.

"Changing monarchs would definitely throw everything into turmoil, both here in Evia and among our allies. It's an odd situation, to be sure," Queen Clarisse eventually agreed. "Perhaps your father would be content to act as an advisor, instead of reclaiming the throne. If Sam agrees to that, of course. I just feel bad that he wasn't ever supposed to have the responsibility, but got thrust into the midst of it anyway. And at such a young age."

"He's a good king," Ian reassured them. "He's grown up well and has a good head on his shoulders, especially considering the circumstances. I check in on him from time to time with the magic mirror."

"Can we see him now?" Clarisse's voice held a note of frightened hope as she curled her fingers into her discarded napkin. "It's been so long."

"Of course." Ian leaned over the table, scooting the mirror toward them as he asked it to show them Sam.

A young man came into view, sitting in a grand study. He was bent over several documents, reading them before signing the bottoms with a small, neat signature.

Clarisse's breath caught. Her knuckles turned white as she gripped Samuel's arm. He shook her off to wrap his arms around her, pulling her close while they watched their youngest son together for the first time in a decade.

"I can't believe it's really him," the queen choked out. "Our little boy, all grown up. Curse that evil bitch for making us miss it."

Samuel rubbed her back, unable to respond. Tears swam in his eyes.

"I'm sorry that I didn't come show you with the mirror," Ian apologized. The corners of his eyes were pinched together. "It never even occurred to me that you might still be alive in there. I had hope at first, but when you didn't shift back with the rest of us on that first solstice, I thought you were gone forever."

Queen Clarisse waved her hand in front of her face, trying to keep the tears at bay. "It's all right. There was no way you could have known. I just missed you both so much..." Overwhelmed with emotion, she broke down. Heaving sobs wracked her frame as Samuel held her close, stroking her hair.

"We'll go to Sedonia as soon as we can, my love," he comforted her. "We can leave in the morning if you want to."

"But Ian- I don't want to leave Ian right away," she protested. "We only just got him back as well!"

"Maman, it's fine! I know that you want to stay, but like Pere' said, it will be safer for you in Sedonia. I'll feel better knowing that you're there, with Sam, heavily guarded against Elavee," Ian said. "Belle and I will join you, at least for a visit, as soon as we can."

"I'll just worry about you two, out here by yourselves," Queen Clarisse fretted.

"You could always send back a guard regiment," Ian reminded her. "It would make you feel better and might even come in handy in case this ogre decides to come after Belle or her sister again."

If he survives Ronan, that is. Ian was a little annoyed at the thought, but brushed it off. *I suppose it doesn't matter who kills him, as long as someone does. He's come after Belle, and now Daphne and threatened Sam. He's too much of a danger to let go anymore.*

Samuel snapped his fingers as an idea struck him. "We'll have him arrested. He's kidnapped the sister of the future queen, after all. That makes him an enemy of Evia, even if he doesn't live here."

Belle's mouth went dry and she sipped the last of her wine. *Future queen... I suppose so, one way or another. I can't breathe.* "I think I need to put Grayson to bed," Belle said softly. "He can't be comfortable like this. Granny, could you please show me to his room?"

Granny Rousseau nodded immediately. They stood together and left the dining room.

"Needed to get away, eh, child?" the old sorceress asked. "It's all a bit much, isn't it?"

Belle gulped in air as she tried to keep herself from panicking. "I just can't believe how much everything's changed in one day. I was looking forward to coming home and working things out with Beast, but then Monique was going to kill me until Ronan came along, and Beast proposed marriage and transformed into Ian. Who I'm not even sure I much liked up until now, plus his parents - the King and Queen of Evia - are secretly alive and want us to go to the capital and have our *royal wedding* there."

She leaned against the wall, cuddling Grayson to her chest. His puppy snores helped to steady her. "On top of all of that, my sister has been kidnapped by a woman who tried to kill me and a man hell-bent on owning me any way he can. Also, I'm holding a baby werewolf, who might end up being my nephew. As though I had any idea werewolves even existed before today, not to mention that my future husband is part fae and any children we have will be, too."

Granny chuckled and patted Belle's shoulder, careful not to wake the sleeping cub. "That sounds like a very long day, my dear."

"I just want to take a bath and go to bed. But I can't because I'll be up worrying about Daphne until I see that Ronan has rescued her safely from Gustav."

"Indeed. I'm anxiously waiting on that news as well, although I'm afraid it might be harder than Ronan is anticipating. Gustav has been quite busy in the woods recently."

She opened a bedroom door and led Belle inside. "I wish I'd been able to speak with him before he left, but I suppose it wasn't meant to be. Gustav has had his cronies bringing weapons, horses, game hunters and the like through my forest, but I'm not sure why. They don't go toward your village, but haven't mentioned the castle, either. I don't even think they could have found it if they'd tried."

"Why not?" Belle asked after she'd gently laid Grayson down. "It's a castle. Surely someone knew of its existence, and I found it easily enough the first time."

"Did you?" Granny raised one eyebrow as she settled onto the settee in front of her fireplace. "Are you sure about that?"

Belle thought back, trying to remember. "I suppose not. Phoebe and I were running from the wolves, and Beast brought us to the castle."

Granny nodded. "Exactly."

"What does that mean, though? I couldn't have ever found it on my own?"

"Part of my counter-curse included a protective spell

that prevented anyone that searched for the castle from finding it, unless they'd been here before or were led by someone who had. I knew that once the story got out, the castle would be robbed immediately, and Ian most likely killed. He didn't have much control over himself those first few years, and it would have been easy for a skilled hunter to pick him off with a bow. I couldn't let that happen, since the curse couldn't have ever been broken if he died."

Shuddering at the thought, Belle whispered, "But he said that a few people did make it in over the years. He chased them off and the stories spread, but a few managed to get past the walls."

"Wanderers and vagabonds, mostly," Granny dismissed. "None that were actively looking for the castle, but I couldn't do as much about someone just wandering by on their way to something else. But the point remains."

"Until today," Belle replied, sick to her stomach. "The curse broke today, so Gustav could find us and attack at any time."

"He doesn't know that. Whatever he's planning, he set into motion weeks ago, so I don't think it has anything to do with coming here directly. He's been out looking for the castle, don't get me wrong, but he never found it, so he's not sure that it even exists."

"The wolves knew where it was," Belle mumbled. "Ronan and Monique both. And Gustav has someone to lead him here, even if the magic was still in place."

Granny's eyes jerked up to meet Belle's. "Who?!"

"Felicity. She used to be a maid here, but she thought she was in love with Beast. She tried to get me out of the way several times, then left when Beast kept saving me. I saw her in the village yesterday and she mentioned that she was there with Gustav, but I didn't realize who she was at the time. I'd imagine that she knows the curse is broken since she's still human."

"That changes things. I think we should check on Daphne."

Belle nodded as she patted her pocket. "Damn. I left the mirror in the dining room."

The edge of Granny's mouth twitched upward in a smile. "That's all right, dear. I think we can manage."

She muttered a few words as she drew a large square on top of the end table nearby. The space inside the square seemed to ripple for a moment, then swirled like the surface of the magic mirror.

"See?" Granny scooted over to let Belle have a closer look. Daphne was, thankfully, on Ronan's back, clinging to his fur as he raced through the woods. Some twenty-odd other wolves ran alongside them, but not all of them looked friendly.

A large gray and white one barreled into Ronan's side, nearly knocking Daphne off. She raised a hand and shouted something unintelligible, sending the attacker careening into the woods. It hit a tree and lay still.

Another wolf sprinted toward them, only to be knocked off course by one of Ronan's pack. Soon enough, running wolves surrounded Ronan and Daphne, snapping at any others who dared come too close.

Ronan stretched his neck out and put on a burst of speed, easily outpacing the other shifters. Belle watched with bated breath as he hurtled through the woods. Once or twice she caught a glimpse of them passing riders on horseback, but none had a chance of keeping up with him.

Eventually he slowed, then stopped. Daphne slid from his back and waited while he transformed, his sides heaving with exertion. Belle leaned back in her seat, averting her eyes when she recalled that Ronan would be stark naked after transforming.

Granny's soft chuckle brought her gaze back to the table-top. Daphne was pushing Ronan to the soft dirt, her lips firmly locked on his as his hands kneaded her rear end.

"Well, then. I suppose that's enough of that." They disappeared. "At least we know she's safe."

Belle blushed and nodded. "Indeed. I'm glad he got her away, and she looks to be in one piece. I hope all of Ronan's pack made it out unscathed as well."

"I'm certain that they did. His wolves are a tough lot."

"I wonder what they did to Gustav. And Felicity."

"Would you like to see?" Granny gestured to the tabletop again. "I can scry them for you, but be warned, the after-math of a werewolf attack is seldom pretty."

Her belly turned and she shook her head, a little nause-ated by the idea. "No, thank you. We saw Daphne's escape, so I don't think we really need to know any more. Ronan said that he'd deal with Gustav and I trust him."

"That's probably for the best. You can always ask when they get here tomorrow, if you decide that you want to know."

"Exactly." Belle stood, brushing her palms across the front of her dress. "Thank you for letting me watch that with you, but now I think I'm going to get Beast and retire. It's been an exceptionally long day."

"Of course," Granny said with a twinkle in her eye. "Have a wonderful rest of the evening. Come see me in the morning if you need any ointment or bath salts to soak away the discomfort."

Confused, Belle tilted her head. "What would I need ointment for?"

Granny laughed softly as she showed Belle to the door.

"Oh, I think you'll find out, my dear. But I'm sure he'll make it a delightful experience, if he hasn't already. He had that reputation for a reason, you know. Goodnight, Belle."

The door clicked shut and Belle stood in the hallway alone. "What on earth..." Suddenly she blushed, realizing what Granny meant. "I meant retire as in go to sleep! Granny!"

Soft laughter came from under the door, but nothing else.

Still blushing, Belle made her way back to the dining room. Thankfully it was empty aside from Ian, who stood as she came in.

"There you are, my beauty. I was wondering where you ran off to." A covered plate sat on the table before him. "You missed dessert. Cook made cheesecake."

"It sounds delicious, but can we take it to our room? I'm afraid that I'm about to fall asleep on my feet."

He grinned and scooped her up against his chest. "We can't have that happening," he murmured into her ear. She shivered as he nipped at the lobe, then kissed it.

"Mmm, thank you. But I truly am exhausted. It's been a long day."

"I know, love. We'll go to bed soon." Ian squeezed her rear as she tried to wiggle down. "Stop that unless you want me back under your skirts before we even make it to our room," he commanded.

Passion stirred in her belly, but it was quickly overwhelmed by her exhaustion. "How about tomorrow morning, instead?"

His laughter rang through the room as he set her on her feet. "Definitely. Do you want to see how Daphne is doing? Ronan should be getting to her soon."

Images of Daphne shoving a very naked Ronan to the

ground beneath her flashed through Belle's mind. "Uh, no. I don't think that's a good idea. I mean, she's safe."

A lifted eyebrow and soft, "Oh?" were his only response.

"Granny did a scrying thing on the table in her room and we saw them escaping. I didn't see what happened to Gustav or Felicity, but Daphne is safe now. That's what's important."

"Why do you sound so strange, then?"

Belle blushed. "We stopped watching when they, ah, stopped to celebrate." *Please don't make me spell it out.*

Ian laughed again. "Leave it to them to barely escape death, then take a break for sex in the middle of the woods. I have a feeling that we'll be getting a niece or nephew shortly."

"It honestly wouldn't surprise me," she agreed. "But by that logic, we already have one. Grayson."

"That's not quite what I meant." He opened the door to their room for her.

"I know, but one can hope. Daphne would have told me if there was anything serious between them."

"She didn't even tell you that he existed, you had to find out on your own," Ian said as he watched Belle undo her laces. "So maybe it's just a fling. Here, allow me to do that."

He made quick work of the ribbons, smiling when her bodice opened enough for him to pull it apart. He scooped her breasts into his palms, reveling at their smooth weight.

Belle gave a tiny purr of enjoyment as he rubbed his thumbs over her nipples.

"They're just so perfect," Ian breathed. "Do you have any idea how many times I wished I had hands, actual hands, to do this with? Instead of having to be careful of my claws scratching you, or my pads being too rough?"

He squeezed each one, fascinated by the way his fingers

curled around her curves. Her nipples puckered under his ministrations and he groaned, then leaned down to lick each ruched peak.

Her exhaustion fading to the background, Belle ran her fingers through his hair, tugging in encouragement. Ian released her to wrap his arms around her legs, lifting her as he straightened. Locking her legs around his chest, Belle pressed against him as he kissed his way across the sensitive underside of each breast.

"Does this mean you're not so tired after all, my little beauty?"

She couldn't stifle a moan as he gently nipped at her, scraping his teeth across her skin. "I suppose you could persuade me to stay up a few more minutes."

Ian flashed her a grin before settling his mouth above one nipple and giving it a hard suck. She gasped, clenching his hair in her palms.

"I'll see what I can do," he replied, laying them on the bed. It was a long time before they went to sleep that night.

10

ound, pound, pound.

"Ughhh," Belle groaned, pulling the covers over her head. Warmth pressed against her back and she cuddled into it, running her hands across Beast's shoulder. Bare skin met her touch and she jerked away in surprise.

Everything flooded back after a moment and she propped herself up on one elbow, content to lie there and look at Ian for a moment. His wide chest, almost as wide as Beast's, rose and fell in a steady rhythm. The clefts between his muscles cast shadows across his body.

I want to lick them. She giggled at the thought, then scooted closer to do just that.

Someone pounded on the door again. Ian gave a sleepy growl as he rolled over. "This had better be good," he muttered.

"They woke me a minute ago, too," Belle said quietly. "I suppose it must be important to keep banging like that."

"It had better be." He rolled over on top of her, nuzzling her throat and covering her jaw with sloppy, playful kisses. She giggled as he ended each one with a smack of his lips.

"Don't move," he ordered as the banging started back up. "I have plans for you."

Belle grinned and wrapped her arms and legs around him, holding him still to begin her own onslaught of pecking kisses. Ian groaned as she sprinkled them across his chest, then pressed his already-hard cock against her center.

She immediately got wet.

"You're killing me," he groaned. Belle wiggled against him.

"I know you're awake, I can hear you muttering in there!" Daphne called through the door.

"Daphne! They're here!" Belle immediately released Ian and scooted off the bed. Running for the armoire, she threw on a dressing gown. "Hurry up! I want to see her!"

Ian laughed as he pulled on pants. Belle was already halfway to the door before he even found a shirt. He was still shoving his arms into the sleeves as Belle jerked the door open, revealing Daphne and Ronan on the other side.

The sisters crashed together, hugging tightly.

"Are you okay?" Belle demanded. "I was so afraid Gustav or Felicity would hurt you!"

"I'm fine. Truly. Gustav wasn't there much and when he was, Felicity actually kept him away from me."

"Really?"

Daphne nodded. "She said something about you being right about him, and that he shouldn't be left alone with me tied up."

"She protected you?" Belle asked, confused.

"The entire time. She has a plan, but I'm not sure what, or why. But yes, she kept him away from me, for what it's worth." Daphne shrugged. "She had a bruise on her cheek and Gustav was giving her that attitude - you know. How he used to treat Aubree after he was done with her and didn't care what happened to her."

"He actually tied you up?" Ian demanded. Ronan growled. "How did you get free? It looked like you were just locked in the shed when we checked on you."

"The fucker tried," Ronan replied. "But he doesn't know our Daphne as well as he thought. She cursed him into coughing uncontrollably for the first several days that she was there."

"Felicity untied me once he was too afraid to come near."

"*Our Daphne?*" Belle whispered to her sister.

Daphne rolled her eyes. "It doesn't mean anything, so don't overreact. Even if it did, like you're one to talk. Only in your dressing gown and Ian's still not properly clothed. I'm assuming you had a good night?"

Belle giggled. "I was about to have a good morning too, before you so rudely interrupted. We're engaged now, you know."

"Ha. Like not being engaged stopped you before."

"Meh. He's it for me, Daph. Even as Beast."

"I'd say especially as the beast," she teased. "But congratulations on your engagement, I'm very happy for you, sister."

"From the way Ronan was going on in front of Papa, it sounds like you're not far behind," Belle shot back. "You should have seen him - stark naked after shifting and practically declaring himself your lover. He has no shame! He even wiggled *it* at us before he put on pants!"

"Ha! He is rather proud of it, the cad. Werewolves have absolutely no sense of modesty, but that doesn't mean you should expect a ring on my hand any time soon. We're just friends."

"Just friends." Belle raised her eyebrow as she recalled the way Daphne had kissed him and pushed him beneath her after the rescue. *What she does with Ronan is her business, but that looked a lot more intimate than just friends to me.* "Still, I thought Papa's eyes were going to pop out of his head."

Daphne threw back her head and laughed. "I bet he was scandalized."

Belle nodded, laughing as she let Daphne go.

"What are you two whispering about over there?" Ronan asked. "I don't trust her when she does that laugh," he muttered to Ian.

"Just how you scandalized Belle and my father with your naked wiggling of certain body parts."

Ian scowled as Ronan laughed.

"You were naked in front of my fiancee?"

Ronan shrugged. "The situation called for it at the time." Ian tensed.

"He had just saved me from Monique - his sister, and her mate. They were lying in wait at Granny's house to try to find out who had Grayson. Ronan made them leave me alone, then shifted into a wolf and gave me a ride to Papa and our cart. I had sent them ahead to tell you what happened to me, in case I didn't make it."

"So, why was he naked?"

"Because I don't exactly carry around an extra set of clothes when I'm saving lovely ladies from being eaten alive," Ronan retorted. "The idiot horse had taken a turn too fast and thrown a wheel off the cart, so I put it back on and repaired it as best I could at the time. Then I escorted your beloved and her father to the safety of your castle while wearing a pair of his pants. Which made *my* crown jewels ache from lack of blood flow, so really, you're welcome."

Ian nearly growled and Belle could just see Beast snapping his teeth in irritation.

"I truly don't think we would have made it back without him, my love," she said, laying her hand on his arm. "He didn't mean anything by it, other than being funny. He was a perfect gentleman otherwise."

Daphne harrumphed in Ronan's general direction.

He spread his hands out in front of him and shrugged. "Don't act so surprised. I'm always a perfect gentleman."

She just rolled her eyes.

"So, back to Felicity and Gustav," Belle said. "Granny told me that he's been having hunting parties coming through the woods, along with a lot of weapons. Do you have any idea what he's planning? Or why he wants Beast and I so badly?"

"I'm not calling you that, by the way," Ronan interjected. "What's your real name?"

"Sebastian. But I go by Ian."

Ronan nodded.

"From what I understand, the evil bitch convinced him that there's treasure here at the castle. A lot of it. And that he can have it, as well as Belle, if he just kills the beast," Daphne said. "He told me basically the same story he told you that day, Belle, but he was frustrated because he hasn't been able to find this place on his own. So he was about to give up when Felicity showed up as a candlestick or some nonsense. She scared the daylights out of him but convinced him to keep going with the plan, then got a little more than she bargained for when she transformed on the solstice. I think she's regretting it, but the damage is already done. Gustav will kill her if she tries to back out now, and the other shifter pack knows how to find the castle anyway. So it's a moot point."

"I wonder what Elavee gets out of this," Belle mused aloud. "Surely it can't just be because she hates your father."

Ian shrugged. "There's no telling with fae. It could be that, or jealousy, or something else."

"Or perhaps, I don't know, the fact that you're supposed to be the crown prince?" Daphne said in a dry tone. "People do atrocious things for a chance at a throne all the time."

"I doubt it. There's a lot more background to it than that," Ian replied as he ran one hand through his hair. "If she were merely human I'd believe that was all, too. But Sam is the king, so why even bother with us? Everyone thinks I'm already dead. Why not just kill me in the beginning, instead of cursing me?"

"Leverage?" Belle guessed. "She might not have wanted to kill you right away, since she might need to use your curse against Sam one day? If she's not already - promising to cure you if he does something for her."

Ian shrugged. "Again, she's fae. There's nothing that Sam could do for her that she couldn't do for herself. It has to be personal."

Daphne shrugged. "If you say so. It sounds like she wants power, and I don't know of a better way to get it than through a crown."

"It's too bad we can't see her with the mirror and figure out what she's up to." Ronan looked down at his fingernails. "Gustav wasn't at the camp when I got Daphne out of there, so he's still probably planning something. Felicity wasn't there, either."

"Why didn't you say so before?" Ian demanded as he grabbed the mirror from the settee. "We assumed that you'd handled that."

"Well, you know what they say about assuming," Ronan replied with a grin. "I wasn't about to leave Daphne there just to go looking for them. He's your problem, not mine."

Daphne scowled at him. "I'm helping. Belle's my sister. So that makes it my problem, too."

"You don't have to do that," Belle interjected. "I don't want to fight with him, and Beast's parents are going to send a guard back as soon as they get to Sedonia."

"The guard won't make it in time." Ian turned the mirror around to let them see Gustav at his lodge in town. He was standing on a table, a bow in one hand and sword in the other. They could all hear him promising the huntsmen and his other cronies riches beyond belief if they just helped him to storm the castle and kill the monster inside.

"We need to get your parents out of here, now," Belle whispered in shock. "Grayson and Granny Rousseau, too." She looked at her sister across the room. "Maybe we should all just leave."

"And leave the castle completely open?" Daphne shook her head. "No. Gustav is an ass and a bully. I'm not letting him ransack your home just because he wants a few gold coins."

"But it's not just Gustav we're talking about. Elavee is on his side - you remember, the enchantress that cursed everyone here to begin with? She's so very powerful, and I don't want anyone else tangled up with her that doesn't need to be," Belle protested. "There's no point putting yourself at risk when I'll just worry about you."

"I think I'm the one that will be worrying about you, big sister. Don't forget, I'm not exactly untrained, myself."

Ronan exchanged a glance with Ian. Both men nodded.

"You're both leaving with Granny and Grayson," Ronan ordered. "Today. Within the hour."

"I'll go let Maman and Pere' know that you're going to Sedonia with them, and you're all leaving as soon as possible. You can take the second coach so that there's room for everyone. We'll handle the rest of this from here, so start packing, Belle."

"What?!" she sputtered in outrage. "You don't get to just tell me what to do like I'm some kind of servan-"

He cut her off with a kiss. Hard, dominating and all business, he held her tight against his body and kissed her with a desperation that left her reeling.

"I can't lose you again," he finally muttered against her lips. "Curse or no curse, you're all that matters to me, and it was hell being apart from you while you were in the village. I had no idea if we were going to be able to work everything out, and I missed you every second that you were gone. I'm not going to be able to function if I have to worry about you here, in that bitch's sights. This needs to end, and I need you safe somewhere else to make that happen."

He kissed her again, gentler this time. "I would never try to tell you what to do, or treat you with anything less than my utmost respect, unless it was absolutely necessary. You mean too much to me."

She melted. "You mean everything to me, too," she whispered back. "I don't know that Daphne will agree to it, but I'll go."

"I'd honestly feel better if she's there for all of you. You, your father, my parents, Grayson and Granny will all need someone to make sure that you actually get to Sedonia safely, and she's the best choice. I think Ronan and I will both feel better if she's with you."

Belle glanced across the room to see her sister and the shifter having a similar conversation. Daphne looked angry, but was nodding anyway.

"I'm going to go tell my parents what's happening. Will you please pack a bag so you can leave as soon as possible?"

Belle smiled and hugged him at the request. "Since you asked nicely."

Ian laughed, then kissed the top of her head. "Thank you, my beauty. I love you."

"I love you, too."

He let her go and headed for the door. Ronan glanced over at him and gave a slight nod.

"Wait! Belle, come here!" Daphne screamed.

Belle looked over in confusion, but didn't move. "What?"

Daphne's hands glowed as she began a spell, but it was too late. Feminine laughter filled the room from out of nowhere. Panic welled up in Belle's chest as the sound slid over her like an oil, coating her senses in dread.

"Beast?" she whispered. He reached out for her, too far away.

Disembodied arms wrapped around her from out of nowhere, pulling her backwards. Daphne threw something at her, but Belle couldn't catch it before she was gone, landing somewhere in the woods.

11

"**B**elle?! BELLE!" Ian bellowed her name as he
charged across the room. No one answered.

"Where is she?" he demanded, whirling on
Daphne. "Where did she go?!"

Daphne was still staring at the spot her sister had disappeared from. "I... I don't know. Where's Granny?"

"I don't care about Granny Rousseau right now!" Ian
roared. "Bring Belle back, now!"

Daphne gave the tiniest flinch as she was jolted out of
her shock, earning Ian a glare from Ronan.

"I don't care what you care about, Granny is the best shot
we have at helping Belle right now! If you're too stupid to
see that, then there's nothing I can do for you!" she shot
back. "I can't just bring Belle back on my own!"

She whirled and stomped out the bedroom door.
"Which room is hers?" she yelled from the hallway.

An older, portly woman beamed at Daphne from the
end of the hall. "Daphne? My dear, it's me, Mrs. Amb-"

Daphne rushed her. Mrs. Ambly took two steps back in
surprise, then smiled happily as Daphne grabbed her arms.

The expression faded as she took in Daphne's pinched eyes and pursed lips.

"Belle's been kidnapped. I need to find Granny Rousseau right away. Which room is hers?"

"Kidnapped? Our Belle? Oh my!" She looked to Ian for confirmation, her face crumbling as he nodded. Mrs. Ambly pointed down an adjoining hall. "Madame Rousseau's door is standing open, about halfway down. Who has Belle?"

"Elavee, the enchantress," Ian said as Daphne ran. Mrs. Ambly waved him on when he would have slowed to say something else to her.

"Go. Get her back, boy. We need her," the housekeeper managed to choke out. "It's lovely seeing you again, though."

"You too, Mrs. Ambly. You too."

"AND THEN SHE WAS JUST GONE!" Daphne exclaimed as Ian walked in. "I threw my talisman to her, but I have no idea if she got it or not. She didn't catch it, that's for sure."

Granny Rousseau stared at the end table before her, muttering different incantations as she drew a square in chalk. Nothing was happening.

"Can you find her?" Ian demanded. "The mirror wouldn't show me."

Granny ignored him and kept muttering, drawing and redrawing her box.

"Someone tell me what's going on!" Ian bellowed. "Where is she? How did she just disappear like that?!"

Ronan grabbed him by the scruff like an errant pup and threw him into a high-backed chair nearby.

"Sit. Stay there and stop yelling until someone tells you what to do," the shifter nearly growled at him. "You're not helping. Granny and Daphne will find her, but they need time to work."

Granny sat back, pale. "Actually, we won't."

"What?!" Ian lurched upright, only to be pushed back down. Ronan pointed at the seat and bared his teeth.

"If you push me one more time, I swear I'll-" Ian threatened as he stood, his chest bumping into Ronan's. Ronan didn't move.

"You'll what, princeling? Nothing. You don't have it in you anymore. And none of this is helping, anyway."

Daphne hurried over, her arms full of parchment, tiny bags of leather and one of Belle's shoes. "Can you divine her on a map? Even if you can't scry her?" she begged.

Granny gave a deep sigh and nodded as she wiped the chalk off of the table. "We can try. But we're working against a fairy here, and a very old and powerful one at that. I might be able to get an idea, but probably can't pinpoint her exactly."

"What exactly happened to her?" Ian asked again through clenched teeth. "How did she just disappear like that?"

"Elavee snatched her through a scrying portal. Much like your mirror, but bigger," Granny finally told him. "My magic protecting the castle must have kept her from doing it before, but stopped when the curse was broken."

"So why not take me, instead? Why Belle?"

"You're protected. There's a magic charm on you to prevent this sort of thing. Your parents, too, from what I understand."

"A charm? Why didn't you put one on Belle?" he demanded. "You should have put it on Belle instead of just us!"

"I would have, except that I didn't do yours," Granny

retorted. "You've always had it. Sam had it from the first time I met him. I didn't even know it existed before I found him in the woods that night, and it's the only reason I thought to put it on Daphne, or Ronan or Grayson. It's a complicated spell, and I haven't had the chance to make one up for Belle."

"I threw her my protection talisman, though," Daphne muttered, looking away from Granny. "It was the only thing I could think of to do."

Granny sighed. "There's no guarantee that will work, and it just leaves you vulnerable. Why did you throw it?"

"I had to do something."

Granny gave her a brief hug. "I understand. I would have tried anything at that point, too."

"What can it do for her?" Ian asked, suddenly grateful for Daphne's quick thinking. "How will it help?"

Daphne shrugged as she stared at the jumbled pile of items on the table. "I don't know. It might make her more resistant to magic, or might make her immune completely. It's supposed to protect me from malicious spells and charms, but since it's specifically tailored to my energy, there's no telling how effective it will be for Belle."

"Can you use it to find her, somehow?" Ronan asked quietly. "Can you scry or divine or whatever for it, in specific?"

Daphne shook her head. "It's immune to that sort of thing. Wouldn't be much good protecting people if someone can just track it wherever it goes." Her head jerked up and she pinned him with a mischievous look. "You might be able to find it though."

Ronan took a step back, his eyes narrowed. Ian rolled his eyes. *He throws me around like it's nothing, but one little slip of a girl can make him retreat? Ridiculous. Then again, she's an enchantress, and Belle's sister. I might be nervous too.*

"What do you mean?" Ronan asked cautiously. "Why would I be able to find it?"

"It's my whistle." She smiled, overly sweet. "If we can just narrow down what part of the woods she's in, I'm sure she'll be blowing that thing to the moon and back, hoping someone in your pack will hear it."

Ronan groaned as he shoved his hands into his hair. "Gods, those things are annoying."

"But effective," she reminded him.

He rolled his eyes. "That's one word for it. But if the Vouret pack is close, they'll hear it too. Which means someone will take it away sooner rather than later, leaving her vulnerable again."

"Then we'd better hurry," Granny said as she spread everything out on the table.

Ian could only stare as she threw powders into the air, muttering enchantments over them as they settled, and occasionally touching Belle's shoe. The old enchantress looked up after a few minutes and simply said, "There."

Daphne leaned in and studied the map. Several bits were liberally coated with dust, but Ian couldn't tell anything else.

"That's a large area to search," Daphne said aloud. "Is the fairy blocking you?"

Granny Rousseau nodded. "This is as much as I could limit it, so it's up to the wolves, now."

"It's far, too. At least an hour and a half, even as fast as Ronan's pack can travel. And that's after we make it to them." Daphne glanced over at him. "Will they go? I know it's a lot to ask after rescuing me just last night."

Ronan crossed his arms over his chest. "They'll go. Or else."

"Can't we just grab her back through one of your portals?" Ian demanded.

Daphne shook her head. "Elavee is blocking Granny from even seeing her, much less touching her. We'll have to bring her back the old-fashioned way."

"Riding a giant wolf isn't exactly old-fashioned," Ronan said with a little snort. "But it will definitely work."

"What about me? I need to be there. I have to help her."

"How?" Ronan scoffed. "I'm all for having a grand plan and people to execute it, but the truth is, you can't keep up. A horse doesn't have the stamina or speed for this kind of ground, and there's no way you're riding me."

Daphne smirked a moment, then sighed. Her shoulders fell as she studied Ian's face. "I know that you want to go. There's no way I'd be left behind either. But don't forget that you're the main target of this whole thing, and you'd be walking right into a trap."

Ian clenched his fists in frustrated rage. "I know."

"Belle would kill me if anything happened to you, especially so soon after the curse has been broken. You finally have a chance to lead normal lives together." Daphne shrugged one shoulder. "Now, if you'd already been irritating her for the last ten years or so, she might not mind so much, but unluckily for you, it's only been a day."

Ian gave her a tight smile. "I'm sure she'll agree in a decade."

"I promise that we'll have her back soon," Daphne swore. "We're going to leave now, Granny. Let me know if you figure out anything else."

Granny nodded, but didn't take her eyes off of Ian.

Ronan and Daphne left, the door closing swiftly behind them.

"Isn't there anything I can do?" Ian nearly begged. "There has to be something."

"That depends on you, my boy. What do you want to do?"

He shot out of the chair and began to pace, a low growl emanating from his chest. "Anything. Save her. Help somehow. I just want her safe."

"Even if that means sacrificing something of yourself? You could be hurt, you know. Killed, even. They are after you, after all."

He slashed a hand through the air, cutting her off. "I don't care about that! Belle is everything to me. I'd do anything for her. I almost wish-" he broke off with a shout, frustrated beyond means.

"Wish what?" Granny asked. She had several of the pouches that Daphne had brought in laid out on the table.

"Wish for the beast again. At least I could take care of her in that form. Beast was strong, and fast, whereas I'm just... human."

"There's nothing wrong with being human."

"I know. I'm glad the curse broke for my parents, Etienne, Mrs. Ambly and the rest. And I never thought I'd say it, but I miss the beast. Belle loved it, and I suppose that after a while, I did, too." He gave a sharp bark of humorless laughter. "I'd especially love to be him right now, going up against a damned ogre."

"But, Ian, you *are* Beast. There was never anything inside of him that's not inside of you, too. The only thing that's changed is your shape."

"I know that, now. For years I thought of it as a separate thing, a monster that the curse created. But it's not. I'm not.

Although the beast's form would be damned handy right about now."

"Are you sure?"

"Of course."

"Even with the setbacks?"

He shrugged. "Any disadvantages would be worth it to save her. I've loved being able to be with her as a man, but I'd rather be with her as the monster than lose her altogether. It's not about me anymore, and she doesn't deserve whatever hell Gustav and Elavee have planned for her. Not to mention Felicity, who could be trying to hurt her as we speak."

Granny nodded and stood. "Good. I can't remake the curse entirely, but I can do something similar. There won't be any breaking this one though. Are you sure you want the beast form with you for the rest of your life?"

Ian's head snapped up and he stared at her, almost afraid to breathe. "Explain."

"I can't give it to you all the time, but I can curse you with his form for a week out of every month, at minimum. You'll have to spend at least that much time as Beast, or your body will force you to change without your control."

"A week? That's all? And I'll stay myself?"

She nodded. "You'll be able to shift forms at will, like Ronan and the other werewolves do. But unlike them, you'll have to do it regularly or you'll lose control of your form until it balances out again."

"And by regularly, you mean a week out of every month?"

"Or more, that's up to you. There are no negative repercussions if you decide to stay longer."

"This doesn't sound like much of a curse to me. More like a blessing, Granny. What's the catch?"

Laughing a little, she shook her head. "You might not think that when you're stuck in Sedonia, locked away from capital life for a week at a time because you can't be seen in public."

Rolling his eyes, Ian reiterated, "Again, sounds like a blessing. What do I need to do?"

"Nothing. Just sit there and I'll handle the rest. But be warned, it might not be pleasant shifting between bodies." Granny pointed to the chair again. "You'll be more or less the same, strength and speed wise, but I can't promise anything exact. I don't know how Elavee cast the original curse, so I'm just doing it my own way."

It didn't take long, just a few minutes of chanting and some random bags dumped over his head. Eventually Granny stepped back and surveyed him.

"Well, it's done. How do you feel?"

He raised an eyebrow and looked down at himself. "Fine. Are you sure that it worked?"

She nodded. "I can't force you to change though, you'll have to manage that on your own."

"How?"

"I don't know, boy. Figure it out. Think of what makes you feel like the beast, what you used to do the most when you were him."

What did I do most? Aside from being terrified of hurting Belle? He stood and paced. *Break things, I suppose. But I don't want to do that here.*

"I need to walk around and clear my head," he muttered. "Thank you for trying, Granny. I appreciate it more than you know."

"Let's hope I did more than try, my dear. Go, figure it out. You'll be able to help her, I'm sure. I'll let your parents know

what's going on, and that you said they should leave immediately."

He nodded, then left the room. Headed for his old suite,
Ian began untucking his shirt on the way. Luckily, no one
was around to try and stop him in the halls. Once in his old
room, he simply stood there and soaked in the destruction.

*It's amazing that she ever saw through the monster I thought
I was supposed to be. This is insanity.* Violence was evident on
every surface of the room. Broken furniture and dishes
littered the floor, the walls were covered in deep claw marks,
and even the once-fine bedding had been shredded.

The place was little better than a rubbish heap.

"This isn't who I want to be, though. I don't think I could
ever transform back into this version of the beast, now that
I've met Belle." He pushed his way through the broken
doors that led to the balcony. The oddest impulse to jump
over the balustrade instead of taking the stairs, like he used
to do as Beast, overcame him.

"I can't do that yet. The last thing I need is a broken
ankle. I won't be any good to anyone then." Still, the
compulsion nagged at him until he compromised by taking
the stairs two at a time down to the garden.

The rich smell of the earth filled his nostrils and he took
a deep breath. *I already miss that, too. I could smell everything
as Beast, hear the slightest noise and nearly taste the air on my
tongue. Everything was so much deeper.*

Inhaling greedy breaths, Ian tilted his head as he heard
the carriage being readied for his parent's departure. *I bet I
could make it there and back before James ever pulls it down the
driveway.*

Focusing on this thought, Ian began to jog. Soon he was
sprinting, running faster than he ever had as a human.

Fur exploded from his pores as he stretched out his

arms, transitioning to all fours. He felt his body shifting, the bones realigning with every stride until he had to stop or fall. Relaxing into the pain, welcoming it as a way to save Belle, Ian closed his eyes and let himself become Beast once more.

12

Once the transformation had stopped and the pain faded, Beast stood. He shook his fur, chuffing with laughter as the tattered remains of his clothes fell around him.

"It's a good thing no one has been in our room to get my old clothes," he mused aloud. "Or I'd be catching up to Ronan and Daphne naked. Which he deserves, after teasing Belle and her father."

He turned and ran back to the Lady's suite, then hopped up to the balcony for old time's sake.

He nearly hit the wall above it.

Shocked, Beast stuck out his paws and braced himself, then swung to the second-story platform.

"I suppose Granny's spell was more effective than we thought." Wicked teeth glinted in the morning sun as he grinned. "Excellent."

He ducked under the doorjamb to go into the room, something he hadn't had to do before, and grabbed a pair of breeches and shirt from the armoire. Pulling them on, he found that they were tight, nearly constrictive whereas before they'd been loose enough to let him move freely.

Beast scowled.

The shirt ripped as soon as he dropped to all fours, but the breeches held, amazingly enough. Snapping his teeth together in irritation, he took the shirt off completely, opting instead for just his light cloak.

Finally ready, he went back to Granny's room, praying she'd still be there.

She was.

Paling as she opened the door, she took a small step back. He bowed low, earning a smile.

"I see you figured it out."

"Indeed. I have one last favor to ask of you, if you don't mind."

"Oh?" she raised an eyebrow and stepped aside, allowing him to re-enter her room.

"I know you can't find Elavee or Belle. But what about Gustav? Or Felicity?"

Granny Rousseau shook her head. "I need something that belonged to one of them to get a feel for their current location. The energy from the belonging will link with the individual, leaving me a sort of trail to go by."

"Hold on." He took off, heading back outside. He made quick time to a shed near the back of the castle, sifting through its contents quickly. A broken chair leg, painted white, yet still recognizable, stood out.

Snatching it up, he ran back to Granny's room.

"What about something that she used to be part of?" he asked, holding the piece out for inspection.

Granny recoiled. "What is that?"

"All of the servants used to be objects, under the curse. Felicity was, for a long time, the chair that this goes to. She tried to drown Belle and I destroyed it, causing her soul to transfer to something else. We never found out what."

"And you kept the chair's pieces?" Granny asked slowly. "Why?"

"We kept the broken pieces of everything. Some would be used as firewood for Cook's stove, or repaired if it was possible. Everything just got thrown into a shed in the back until it could be disposed of. You have to realize, I broke a lot of furniture at first. Some of it had to be repaired out of necessity."

She raised an eyebrow, but nodded without further comment. "All we can do is try." Taking the chair leg from him, she went back to the table with the map and shook it off. All of the powder went into a small bowl, which she chanted over again as she sprinkled it back onto the map.

It condensed into one tiny spot, well within the larger area that Ronan's pack was going to search.

"She's there?" Beast asked.

Granny nodded.

"Can we see her with the mirror?" He set it down on the table, having grabbed it from his room.

She shrugged. "Let's find out."

He picked it up and demanded that it show Felicity. It took a little longer than usual, but eventually revealed a hazy picture of her in a clearing, arguing with someone. Beast bared his teeth when he realized it was Gustav.

Saddled horses surrounded them, and Belle sat against a tree nearby. Her lips were swollen, and her throat had red marks around it. Beast's lips curled back over his teeth.

"No." Felicity shook her head. "Absolutely not. You obviously can't be trusted, considering what I've already seen, and that's not what I agreed to. The enchantress needs her alive, something you don't seem overly concerned with."

"I'd never hurt her," Gustav scoffed. "I love her."

Felicity raised an eyebrow. "Your hand was around her throat. I don't even want to know where the other one was. That's not love, you boorish ass."

His hand was around her THROAT? Where else did he touch her?! I'm going to rip him apart! How dare he hurt Belle! Beast nearly roared his fury into the small bedroom, but somehow restrained himself. Granny Rousseau patted his arm.

Gustav's brows drew together as he stood straighter, rising to his full height. He stepped forward, his chest bumping Felicity's.

She didn't move.

"You think you can stop me?" he snarled. "Belle belongs to me. She's always been mine, whether she wants to admit it or not. This whole thing with your former master is nothing but a ploy to make sure I come for her."

"You truly have lost your mind, haven't you?" Felicity shook her head. "She doesn't want you, Gustav. I'm amazed any woman would."

He grabbed her arm, then stopped, his eyes widening in surprise. "You wouldn't dare."

Felicity gave him a semblance of a smile, a mere twisting of her lips. Her free hand held a curved dagger, its point digging into his lower belly where his leather vest had risen up.

"Don't think I won't gut you here and now," Felicity hissed. "People like you are what's wrong with the world."

Gustav let go and stepped back. Felicity went with him. A few hunters nearby watched with amusement. "I didn't want to admit it, but you are everything I've always hated. More so than Ian ever was. The world would be better off without you."

Gustav's shoulders tensed and he raised one hand like he was going to hit her. She dug in the blade a little deeper.

He laughed and leaned down, trying to kiss her instead. She dodged, hissing like a cat. Blood dripped from the dagger's blade. Watching the red stain spread gave Beast a macabre sense of delight.

"You think you're still in love with him? And that he'll eventually love you back?"

She glanced away, toward Belle.

"Then why do you care about what I do with Belle? You need her out of the way before your precious prince will even look at you. Not that he'll have much of a chance before his head is mounted on my wall."

Felicity's eyes narrowed as she pulled the dagger from his skin. "He's going to eat you alive, and I'm going to enjoy it. Now stay away from us." She turned and walked away, heading in Belle's direction. The image on the mirror faded instead of following her.

"Why did it stop? I want to see Belle up close," Beast growled. "She looked hurt."

"Whatever spell Elavee cast to keep us from scrying Belle directly must have prevented the mirror from working anymore. It probably has a range, and Felicity was outside of it when we asked to see her."

"It looks like they're moving her. But where?" he demanded. "I can't rescue her without being seen if they're moving."

Granny studied the map. "We need to speak with Daphne and Ronan. Tell them to bring the pack here instead."

"What?" Beast roared. "And just leave Belle out there alone?"

"I don't think she'll be out there long," Granny replied

curtly. "Look at the map. This path comes straight to the castle." She looked up, glaring at Beast. "Get your parents out of here, now. And ready whatever defenses this heap has left. They're coming for you."

THE CARRIAGE ROLLED through the side gate with Clarisse and Samuel a mere thirty minutes later, despite her strenuous objections. They agreed to take a lesser-travelled back road and Granny Rousseau sent a message ahead to Sam that they were coming.

He'd squinted at the paper that she put through the magic mirror, his brow furrowed with confusion.

"*Trust me, child. They're alive, along with your brother, and the curse has been broken. Only tell Rumsfeld, and prepare an escort to meet them. I think they'll need it,*" she wrote out.

"Why Rumsfeld? Why not all of the advisors?" Ian asked, back in his human form. "Do you think there's a spy in court?"

Granny shrugged as she readied another spell. They sat together in the dining room, which had become the main hub for planning defenses. "I don't know for certain, but there are a few people I've seen pop up from time to time. Courts usually have their little intrigues and such, and until they're ready to make a formal announcement, it's best to keep your parents' return private."

Ian nodded. "That's understandable, for now. We have other things to worry about, as long as Maman and Pere' are safe."

"My Lord," Etienne greeted them. He beamed at Ian, his wide smile a permanent fixture since he was reunited with his master a little while earlier. "The gates are all barricaded and traps are being set in the forest beyond."

"Excellent," Ian said. "I doubt that we catch many of the werewolves, or contain them for long, but the hunters and their dogs might be a different story. Let's just hope that Ronan's pack can deal with the other werewolves."

"I still don't understand why they would work with Elavee," Mrs. Ambly tutted. "We've never had any issues with them, much less even known that they existed until recently. Is this all because of this one little boy?"

"I don't know." Ian studied the list of fortifications they were working on. "You'd have to ask Ronan. He'll be here soon. Either way, we need to keep Grayson safe."

The housekeeper nodded. "I have the core suite ready for him."

"I'll be checking on him periodically," Granny Rousseau said matter-of-factly. "Daphne will handle things on the outside and I'll take the inside if it comes to that. These old bones can't handle the stresses of battle anymore."

I wonder if she's actually been in battles before? Ian thought. *It wouldn't surprise me.* She whispered a spell over several long, thick vines that were laying across the table and one rose up, twisting through her fingers. *I'm just glad she's on our side.*

"Put this outside the walls," she instructed Etienne. "Two or three sections on every side. Water them well and stand back. Leave us a few for inside the grounds as well."

He nodded with a hard swallow. The vines writhed under his hands as he picked them up and hurried outside with them, looking definitively nervous.

"Mrs. Ambly, if you would be so kind as to go get the stable boys. I have a job for them as well."

"What about me?" Cookie asked as he stood in the

doorway to the kitchen. "I would like to help as well. Especially against the bitch that took so many years away from us."

Granny paused a moment, her eyes glittering as she appraised him. "That's what I like to hear. Now then, how do you feel about fire?"

The slow grin that spread across the cook's face couldn't be described as anything less than euphoric. "Fire is my specialty, madame."

Ian sat back, shocked as a long-forgotten detail came back to him. "Cookie, weren't you part of my father's royal guard when I was a boy?"

Cook nodded. "Indeed, Master."

Granny raised an eyebrow. "So this isn't anything new to you."

"I've been around long enough to know how it works, madame. Please, allow me to assist you in any way that I can."

"Let's see what all you've got in that kitchen. I'm sure there must be a few things we can use to drum something up."

He bowed as he extended an arm and they left together.

"Well, then. I suppose I'll just send James to the kitchens," Mrs. Ambly said in an amused tone. "Who would have thought."

Ian nodded, then went back to the list. *Is this enough? I know Daphne will be able to use some magic, and we'll have Ronan's pack at our side, but is it really going to be enough to get Belle back safely? And what does Elavee want with her in the first place?*

∾

BEAST TOOK A DEEP BREATH, fighting to keep his temper under control. Perched atop one of the towers, he had a clear view of Gustav and Elavee's forces.

There weren't many of them, but from what Beast could tell, they were organized. Massive wolves crept through the trees, scouting ahead of the hunters on horseback. A long-haired woman rode beside Gustav, sitting astride and pointing at things. Everyone shifted around her, clearly taking her orders, and formed a ring.

She dismounted, allowing Gustav to lead her horse away. He came back leading the one that Belle was riding, her hands tied to its pommel.

Beast snarled. Masonry cracked beneath his hands and he shook beneath the amount of effort it took him to stay hidden instead of running down there and snatching her away.

"I know. We'll get her back, I promise," Daphne said beside him. "She'll be fine."

But even Daphne gasped as Elavee pulled Belle to the ground beside her and lifted her hands, summoning a huge tree from beneath them.

It wrapped sturdy branches around Belle as it grew, effectively caging her in its boughs and taking Elavee into the sky along with them. The wolves, hunters and their horses scattered for a moment, shocked as well.

Gustav simply stood there, watching.

"Well, fuck." Beast ground his teeth together. "We'll have to go out there and get her. There's no way to rescue her from here."

"If the bait is obvious, it's obviously bait," Ronan murmured from Daphne's other side. "They're clearly not going to be moving her until someone wins. She's safe there for now, but who knows what that tree will do if someone approaches it?"

A bird flew close to the tree, investigating the new plant. It whipped a branch through the air, knocking the bird to the forest floor in a puff of feathers.

"That. Apparently, *that* is what it will do." Daphne's voice was strained, but Beast could hear a note of jealousy as well. He scowled.

She glanced his way, but didn't say anything else. They all watched as Gustav shouted something to his hunters and they came forward, all armed with swords and bows. It only took a few moments before several of them were climbing trees as well, setting up their quivers within easy reach and pulling bowstrings tight.

"I suppose that's it then," Ronan muttered. "We should probably get moving on this before they plan any more little surprises."

Beast nodded. "Are your wolves in place?"

"They have been for an hour now."

Beast nodded in the afternoon light. "Daphne, if you wouldn't mind." He watched while Granny's pet vines filtered through the trees, silently making their way toward the hunters perched in the branches.

Daphne took a deep breath. "All right, then." Her voice barely shook. "Good luck to us all."

13

Daphne's whispered words were snatched away by the wind, but their effects were clear. Fire sprang up along the outer edges of the castle walls, singeing the fur and flesh of anyone standing too close. Ronan's wolves howled as they closed in from behind, trapping Gustav's forces against the keep.

Gustav stood in his stirrups, barking out orders to anyone that would listen. Several arrows flew through the air as the archers began to rain down death from above.

They stopped after just a few draws, Granny's enchanted vines pulling tight around wrists, arms and bodies, rendering them useless and knocking most of the quivers to the ground below. But only for a moment. Elavee raised her hands and the vines withered, dragging two archers to the ground as they fell.

Daphne countered, summoning a stiff wind that rocked the forest. Pine needles flew at the remaining archers like tiny arrows themselves, zinging through the air and making the humans duck for cover. Explosions went off in the forest as wolves or hunters got too close to the pressure-sensitive traps rigged up by Cookie and Etienne.

"Let's hope our pack remembers where all of the traps are," Daphne murmured, never taking her eyes off of Elavee. "I couldn't stand to lose anyone in this."

"They'll remember," Ronan replied. "They'll all be fine. We're a resilient lot."

"Good."

Shifting her hands, Daphne redirected the wind to pick up at the base of the fire, blowing cinders and ashes into the mix. The enchantress countered, and lightning crackled through the air. A torrential downpour began, soaking everything within moments.

Beast could barely make out Elavee's laughter from the tower. "She's enjoying this," he growled. "That bitch is having fun while Belle is terrified."

Belle's birdcage-like enclosure swung from its tether in the tree. They could clearly see her sprawled out on the floor against one side, clutching the branches.

"We'll get her. But we have to take care of the rest of them first," Daphne promised. "I hate this just as much as you do." They all watched for a second while Cookie, James and Etienne fired arrows through the bolt-holes in the castle wall, taking out their share of attackers.

"Well, maybe it's time someone made Elavee hate it, too."

Daphne nodded and set her jaw. "I'll try to distract her. Do you think you can make it up there without getting bashed to smithereens?"

"With pleasure." Beast leapt from their tower to a nearby, but lower balcony, then kept jumping until he reached the ground.

"Gustav is still looking for him," Ronan said. "I'll go, too. I owe that bastard after what he did to Grayson, anyway."

Daphne nodded again, only now looking away. "Ronan-" she paused. "Just be careful."

He flashed her a smile and slapped her rear end before transforming into his wolf. A few leaps and he was gone, taking the same path down that Beast had.

"Well, then." Daphne concentrated, blasting the clouds above them with cold. Elavee's rain turned to sleet, then hail, pelting her with marble-sized chunks of ice. The enchantress raised her arms over her head in surprise, glaring toward the castle towers.

Suddenly, she grabbed the branches closest to her. The magic tree shook as Beast and Ronan attacked from below, having leapt over the magically flaming walls with little hesitation. They made it to the base with little contest and began climbing, ignoring the tree's efforts to knock them back down.

Beast ducked and snarled as arrows flew at them, embedding into the tree's bark and enraging it. The few archers that had kept their seats in the surrounding trees took turns firing at Beast and Ronan, then trickled to a stop.

Beast hazarded a look around to find several bodies on the ground, Cook's flamboyantly painted arrows sticking out of them. He roared his thanks, and Cook kept shooting, trying to help where he could.

Beast got to Belle's cage first and clawed at it, desperately trying to make a hole big enough for her to fit through. She helped, slicing through vines with a dagger that had been strapped to her thigh.

But no matter how quickly they destroyed the tree, the branches kept regrowing, sealing her in even tighter.

"No! Beast, look out!" Belle screamed. She shoved the dagger into its sheath and lunged for him.

An arrow pierced his side. He roared in outraged pain, nearly falling from the tree. Belle grabbed his paw from inside the cage, and Ronan bit into his cloak, trying to keep Beast from falling.

An enchanted limb came sweeping in, smashing into Beast's other side. Pushed to his limits, he dug into the cage, ripping open an entire corner at once. Belle leaped through the hole, locking her arms around Beast's neck as he let go of the cage and half-fell, half-climbed down.

Beast landed heavily, favoring his side. Belle slid from his back and pressed her hands against the hole the arrow had left. Another arrow drove into the ground beside them.

Gustav rode toward them from behind a nearby copse of trees. A demented smile spread across his face as he raised his bow again, preparing for the final shot.

"I told you this was how it would end, Belle. His death is your fault!" Gustav shouted. Belle screamed as he pulled the arrow back.

Felicity's horse ran into Gustav's, nearly knocking him from his saddle. The arrow flew wide as he dropped his bow. He whirled in fury, backhanding the smaller woman into the dirt. She rolled, dodging his horse's hooves as a huge wolf suddenly appeared beside her.

It sank its teeth into Gustav's arm, dragging him from the saddle. Belle recoiled as she recognized it.

"Monique," Daphne whispered as she watched from the rooftop. "Be careful, Monique." She sent the werewolf a quick wave of healing energy as Ronan joined her in the fray, then focused on Elavee again. The enchantress had created a cover of flame twisting in the air that melted Daphne's hail in little puffs of steam.

A wolf sailed over the wall, one that Daphne didn't recognize. Several more followed. Cursing, Daphne tried to push them back with the wind.

She needn't have worried. Granny Rousseau stood on the front steps of the castle, surrounded by the garden statues and gargoyles from the roof. One snap of her fingers had them spreading out in lines between the enemy werewolves and the front door, where they waited.

Lightning struck the tower closest to Daphne's hiding place, making her flinch. Narrowing her eyes, she sent her own flash back at Elavee.

PLEASE BE OKAY, please be okay, Belle silently chanted as she pressed Beast's cloak against his side. The arrow was out, dislodged on the way down the tree, but the wound bled in a steady stream. Ronan and Monique snapped and snarled, keeping Gustav busy for the time being.

"Go to the castle," Beast ordered, pushing her toward the wall. "You shouldn't be out here."

"But what about you?!" She shook her head. "I'm not leaving you like this! And I can't get over the wall without you, anyway. You have to get back inside - Elavee is only here because of you."

"I'm not running away!"

"Good," Gustav interjected. "Because I'm the one that's here for you. That fairy bitch promised I could keep her," Gustav pointed at Belle with his broken bow, "and mount your head on my wall."

Belle watched in mute horror as Gustav threw the bow behind him, the pieces nearly hitting Felicity's inert form.

Monique lay near her, panting and bleeding heavily from several wounds.

Ronan was on his feet, but was busy snapping and fighting with two other wolves that had come to Gustav's aid.

What am I going to do? They're all so much stronger than me. But I won't let him hurt Beast any more. Belle hugged Beast's side, taking a deep breath against his fur as she fingered the dagger that Felicity had wordlessly strapped to her leg. *I love you so much, my prince. Please understand.*

Pushing away from him, she turned to Gustav. "You can have me," she said to the hunter. "I won't fight you anymore, if you just let them live. But if you hurt them, you'd better kill me too, because I'll never stop trying to escape you."

Beast roared. Grabbing Belle around the waist, he hauled her behind him and dropped heavily to all fours. "You're never touching her again!"

Gustav laughed as he pulled out a large hunting knife. Twirling it around, he lifted his other hand in a mocking, *come on* motion.

Beast charged. Gustav's face contorted for one brief second, twisting with fear as Beast landed atop him, claws ripping through his leather vest.

Gustav recovered quickly, slashing back with his knife.

Belle pulled her own knife out and circled the pair, determined to help if she could.

Elavee's enchanted tree shuddered behind them, twisting in on itself as black rot streaked up the trunk. No one noticed.

Beast roared as Gustav landed a particularly deep cut. Retaliating with a bite, he closed his jaws around Gustav's shoulder and shook, hard.

A deep crack echoed across the short distance to Belle and she gasped as Gustav's head lolled to the side.

"It's over. Thank goodness, it's over." She sank to her knees, overwhelmed with relief.

Beast shook him again for good measure, then tossed him aside when Gustav didn't respond. Beast turned to Belle, his eyes widening as he caught sight of her dagger.

"Are you all right?" he demanded. Belle nodded.

Another crack rang out.

Confused, they both looked back just in time to see Elavee's tree sway, then start to topple over.

"Beast! Run! Grab Felicity and get out of the way! The tree is coming down!" Belle ordered as she grabbed Monique's front paw and pulled as hard as she could. The wolfgirl's eyes snapped open and she shifted back to human form, doing her best to struggle to her feet.

Beast grabbed them both and ran. Belle wrapped her arms around his neck as her stomach dropped when he leapt, vaulting the wall. The tree crashed through a moment later, barely missing them.

Beast fell beneath all of their weight, his wounds finally overwhelming him.

14

"Beast?! Beast, say something!" Belle shouted as she pushed the other women aside. Dread, and disbelief, filled her when he didn't answer. Blood pooled beneath him, dripping from his side.

Grabbing his collar, Belle shook Beast. "Wake up! You have to wake up! Don't you dare leave me now!"

She gathered up a section of her skirt and pressed it against his side. "Ronan! Daphne! Someone help him!"

Tendrils of golden energy snaked their way between her fingers to his exposed flesh. She stared, dumbfounded as the bleeding slowed, then stopped.

He opened his eyes. "Belle?"

"You're alive! Thank God! I thought you were going to die."

He tried to sit up, winced and laid back again. "Of course not. It's not that bad."

Ronan huffed, shifted to human form and sat down beside them. Belle pulled Beast's cloak to the side to reveal several deep stab wounds, along with dozens of cuts and bruises.

"Not that bad, you say? You're a mess," she choked out with a sob. "Did Gustav do all of this?"

Beast shrugged nonchalantly. "It's nothing. I fell in a bush." He gave her a little smile.

"A bush that fought back," Ronan replied with a smile. "I think I got caught up by the same one."

Beast chuffed his soft laughter, but stopped with a groan.

Daphne ran across the courtyard and skidded to a stop beside them. "Let me see your wounds, both of you! I'll have to do this quickly."

Ronan flopped back beside Beast, uncaring that he was completely naked. Daphne stood over them both and spoke quickly. A golden glow, deeper than the tendrils Belle had seen, suffused the air around them, sealing cuts and staunching the blood that still dripped from deeper wounds.

Both creatures sighed in relief.

Daphne threw a pair of pants at Ronan's belly. "Here. Put some clothes on, you heathen."

He smiled up at her. "Don't pretend that you don't love it."

"Ugh. You're entirely too sure of yourself," she retorted. But neither Beast nor Belle missed the affectionate gleam in her eyes. "I have to take care of your sister. She's in bad shape, too. Felicity as well."

Ronan rolled over and pulled on the pants, then followed Daphne to Monique's side.

"Is that better?" Belle asked, stroking the side of Beast's face.

He nodded. "That feels good," he whispered. "What about Elavee, though? And why are we taking care of Felicity?"

Belle sat up and looked around. A few wolves had tried to sneak in through the broken part of the wall, but garden statues were beating them with heavy masonry fists. She shuddered and looked away. Granny Rousseau was making her way across the courtyard to Daphne and Monique. The woods beyond the wall were quiet.

The tree had disappeared entirely, taking quite a few stones from the wall along with it.

"Felicity actually helped me," Belle replied. "I couldn't believe it myself, but she did. As far as Elavee goes, I don't know where she is, but her tree is completely gone. Everyone sort of scattered when you killed Gustav and the tree came down."

"Is he dead?" Beast tried again to sit up, this time successfully. "Are you sure?"

Belle looked back out into the opening and shrugged. "It sounded like his neck snapped, but I can't be sure without seeing his body. He was definitely unconscious, then the tree fell on top of him. I don't see how he could have survived."

"And you? Are you hurt?" Beast demanded as he pulled her close. He began to run his hands over her body, checking for himself.

"I'm fine, you silly man. Or, I guess, beast again." *Why did he transform back? Did he change his mind about me, so the curse was reinstated?*

He grinned at her. "Isn't it amazing? I'm stronger and faster than I ever was before."

"Bigger, too," she agreed. Her heart constricted painfully as she wondered why. "But the curse was broken. Did you change your mind?"

He tilted his head, confused. "About what? I like the

beast form now. It took falling in love with you to learn how, but I don't think I could live without it now. Without either of you."

He... he still loves me. Thank God. She threw herself against his chest, crying onto his shoulder. "I love you too, Beast. So very much."

"Belle, what's wrong? Why are you so upset?" He stroked her back, his large paw almost covering it entirely as he settled her into his lap. "I love you, too. I love you, too." He kept repeating it until she calmed.

"I saw you from up there as Beast again and I was so afraid that you'd changed your mind about me. About us. I thought maybe the curse wasn't broken after all, so you were changed back."

"Oh, Belle. I love you more than anything in the world. More than I could ever find the words to say. I'd never change my mind about you. You're the best thing that's ever happened to me." He shook his head in disbelief. "I was going crazy thinking that Gustav had you and there was nothing I could do to help, so I asked Granny Rousseau to curse me again."

"But you hated being like this. Why would you ask for it back?" She sniffled, confused. "Does this mean you can never be human again?"

"No, I can change whenever I want. Like Ronan and the werewolves." He hugged her close for a moment, then leaned back onto his hands and relaxed. The shift flowed through him, snapping and mending bones and somehow taking the majority of his injuries along with it.

"But how..." she trailed off, unable to believe it. "You're nearly healed!"

Ian wrapped his arms around her again. "I didn't know about that, but I suppose since the transformation involves so much restructuring, it makes sense that a few injuries would be fixed along with it."

She didn't move, just stared at him.

"Why are you looking at me like that?" he asked, suddenly self-conscious. "I thought you'd be happy to have your beast back." *Have I made a mistake? Maybe she doesn't like that form as much as I had thought. Maybe she was just humoring me.*

"I'm thrilled to have you any way I can. I just can't believe that I saw you get shot with an arrow and stabbed less than a quarter of an hour ago, and now you're fine." She ran her palms over his sides and chest in wonder.

He shuddered beneath her touch, his skin heating in the wake of her fingers. He became suddenly aware of her position straddling his hips, her center lined up with his cock.

It immediately got hard.

"Belle, you have to stop that. There are people around."

She threw herself against him and captured his lips with her own. Ian sucked in a breath, then kissed her back with all of the passion, fear and desperation that he'd gone through that day. He poured his heart into her, and she treasured every bit of it.

"I'm not going to make it back to our bedroom if you keep that up," he managed to whisper between kisses. Their tongues danced together as she kissed him again, completely inflamed.

"Then hurry," she replied before sucking on his lower lip, drawing it between her teeth. "I need you. Need to feel how alive, and whole you are. I was so scared."

Still straddling him, Belle ground herself against his cock with tiny movements, too small for anyone else to see, but just enough to drive him wild.

"Fuck. Hold on to me. And hold my pants up," he

ordered. She giggled as he stood, her skirt hiding his rampant erection.

Ian kept kissing her as he stumbled toward the front door, ignoring Ronan's catcalls and Daphne's teasing laughter. They didn't stop kissing as he carried her down the hallway to their room, bumping into walls along the way.

Belle moaned every time they ran into something, Ian's cock pressing just a little more firmly against her slit.

"I think you're doing that on purpose," she eventually whispered. They'd reached the little side hall that led exclusively to their suite, and was empty. Ian lifted her just enough to reach under her skirt, then settled her back where she had been.

"Doing what?" he asked in a wicked voice, low and growly. "This?" He pressed her back against their door and rotated his hips against hers, rubbing against her clit. "Or this?"

He squeezed her ass before dipping his fingers between her lips, finding her soaking wet. They groaned together as he slid his first two fingers deep into her welcoming heat.

"Mmm, my Beast," she moaned, arching her back. He welcomed the invitation and hoisted her up to his mouth, kissing the tops of her breasts.

"Get us into that room, now," Belle ordered.

Ian grinned and slipped his fingers out, relishing the disappointment on her face before he thrust them back in. "Demanding Beauty. I love it."

She gasped, bordering on crying out as he set a hard, fast pace with his hand. "I'm serious, Beast. Open this door right now, or I'm going to climax in the middle of the hallway. And you wouldn't want anyone to walk by and see me, right?"

He growled and bit her breast, just over her nipple.

"You're all mine." Jerking the door open, he twirled them inside, ending up with her back still against the portal.

"Now cum for me," he ordered. His thumb found her clit and pressed against it, rubbing as he added a third finger inside her.

She shattered, screaming his name as she convulsed. Ian pulled her skirt up, tugging it from between them as he dropped his breeches.

His hard cock sprang up between them, rubbing against her sex.

"Yesss..." Belle squirmed against him, coating him in her juices. He gave her a languid thrust, teasing her entrance before slamming home.

Her eyes nearly rolled back into her head as she came again, her inner walls gripping him tightly.

"Fuck, Belle. I don't know how you do that, but don't stop." He drove into her again and again, pressing her back against the door. She clung to him, her legs wrapped around his waist and her hands deep in his hair.

It didn't take long before it was too much, overwhelming Ian with pleasure. He ground against her, crushing her hips against his as he released inside her, filling her with himself.

Their breaths mingled as he stood there, unable to move for a moment. He rested his forehead against hers, then pressed another sweet kiss to her lips.

"That was..."

"Amazing," he finished for her. "I don't know how I'm going to survive you if it's always like this between us. You might finish me off faster than all the rest of our enemies combined."

She giggled, then bit his shoulder. "Don't say that. I'm still scared of losing you from earlier."

"You're never going to lose me. Just accept it. We're in this forever," he said as he carried her to the bed.

"Forever," she agreed, stretching out beneath him.

"Now then, let's get this dress off."

15

Things flowed easily over the next few weeks. Daphne and Ronan had occasionally disappeared to some secluded corner while Granny and Grayson played together. He was, of course, ecstatic to have his Daphne back, but agreed to share her with his daddy after the required three days of having her attention all to himself.

Ian had laughed until he realized that their children would be just as demanding of Belle's time.

Ronan's werewolves took up residence in one of the outbuildings after Monique refused to be stuck in a suite in the castle proper, as she put it. Ronan had just shaken his head and acquiesced, letting her recuperate wherever she wanted.

Felicity was locked in a sickroom, allowed only a few visitors while she recovered from the fight with Gustav. It was at her door that Ian found himself just before leaving for Sedonia.

"Explain to me again why we're being nice to Felicity?

She tried to kill you," he said, grabbing Belle's hand when she went to open the door.

"She did," Belle agreed slowly. "When she was stuck here, thinking that she was madly in love with you and that I was just some throne-chasing bitch come to steal you away from her."

"What?" Ian stared at her blankly. "No one could have possibly thought that was the case. All the more proof that she's out of her mind."

Belle rolled her eyes. "She was trapped as a chair for a decade. Of course she wasn't in her right mind. And then once she got out of here, she ended up with Gustav, of all people. Not exactly an experience I'd wish on anyone, regardless of if they've already happened to share your bed or not."

"What's that mean?" he demanded, hurt.

"Just that Gustav wasn't one to take no for an answer. I tried to warn her about that, but I have a strong feeling she found out on her own. I was wary of her at first too, but she tried very hard to keep him away from me while I was their captive. Daphne said the same thing. Whatever Felicity's reasons were, she protected us both when we needed it the most, and I want to hear why. She even gave me the dagger when no one was looking."

Ian lifted an eyebrow at that. "The one I found under your skirt that night? I always wondered where you'd gotten that thing."

Belle nodded. "She could have easily killed me so many times, my love. But instead she tried to help me. Surely that counts for something?"

Ian let her hand go. "Fine. But if she makes one wrong move toward you, I'm not going to hesitate."

Belle gave him a brilliant smile. "Thank you."

They opened the door to find the room empty, and the curtain fluttering in the breeze. A note sat in the middle of the bed, which looked like it hadn't been slept on in quite some time.

BELLE,

I JUST WANT to say that I'm sorry. I know you probably won't believe me since I'm writing it in a letter instead of telling you in person, or if you'll even read this, but I truly am sorry. I misjudged you in the beginning, and everyone almost paid the price. You loved Ian enough in any form to break the curse, which I see now that I never could have done. On top of that, you took the time and risk to warn me about Gustav, even though I didn't listen to you about that, either.

You were right. He was evil, and I'm glad that he's finally gone from the world. I don't think that anyone but Beast could have done it. Not even Ian. Not even me, on my own. I'm also sorry for my part in bringing Gustav to the castle in the beginning, but I was just so angry. I thought it was Ian's fault that I'd spent ten years as a bloody piece of furniture, even though now I know it wasn't. But by the time I realized that, Elavee already had her hooks in Gustav, filling his head with that treasure nonsense and promising him that you were secretly in love with him, so he was coming for you either way. I figured the best thing to do was stay with them and keep an eye on the situation, to see if I could make amends in some way. I'm glad that I did a little, in the end. He would have hurt you, and Daphne, if he'd had a chance.

You're not anything like I thought. You're not anything like me. I'm sorry that I made things more difficult for you while you were at the castle, and even afterwards. I stuck around for a while as a candlestick, and saw how crazy my actions made Ian. I'll admit that it was entertaining for a little while, but watching him watch you, scared into nearly driving you away, eventually just made me realize how much he needed you. And how much everyone there needed you to break the curse.

So, thank you for sticking it out. Thank you for breaking the curse and giving us back our humanity, even if it's a little worse for wear in some cases. But that's not your fault.

Tell Daphne I said goodbye, and Ian, I suppose. I doubt I'll ever see any of you again, as I'm going to put as much distance between me and that castle as I can. But still. Thank you.

FELICITY

BELLE READ THE NOTE, then handed it to Ian. He scanned it quickly.

"Well. I don't really know what to say about that, except I guess you really can make anyone like you," he teased. There was an odd strain to his voice.

"What's wrong?" Belle asked. "She's gone now. We probably won't see her again."

"I know," he replied. "It just seems strange that she'd write this, then leave. I know you weren't exactly friends, but if she likes you this much and tried so hard to take care of you and Daphne, maybe she wasn't so bad."

"I suppose she didn't feel comfortable staying. Can you really blame her? She thought she was in love with you, and tried to kill me. You, yourself, were just threatening to rip her apart if she so much as looked at me wrong. She deserves a real second chance to be someone else. To lead a life that she chooses, instead of one where it doesn't seem like she's had many options."

Belle leaned against Ian's chest. "I'm proud of her."

"Well, as long as you're happy, I am, too." He kissed the top of her head. "We should really be going though. We have a long trip ahead of us."

"I know," Belle replied. "Your Maman and Pere will be waiting. And I can't wait to meet Sam."

"He can't wait either, my love." Ian gave her a slow kiss. "And I can't wait to tell them the good news."

THE END

*Keep reading for a sneak peak at Sam's story in **The Little Mermaid**, and Daphne's story in **Little Red Riding Hood.***

THE LITTLE MERMAID

by Nikki Dean
Available on Amazon at My Book

CHAPTER 1

Sam

S amuel Morel, the King of Evia, laid back in his tiny sailboat and stared at the stars. The gentle rocking usually soothed his overactive mind, but tonight nothing seemed to be helping.

He rubbed a hand over his face. "I should probably be getting back, then. It wouldn't do any good to have someone notice that I'm not in the castle."

Picking up the oars, he glanced back into the dark water one more time, hoping beyond hope that he'd see it again.

"There you are," he crooned, leaning over the edge. "I was wondering if you were going to come out tonight."

The greenish-blue light flickered far beneath the surface. Sam held his hand over the side of the boat and dropped a little girl's crystal-studded necklace into the water. It twinkled as it sank, reflecting in the strange glow coming from under the waves. Exactly as he'd hoped.

The little light paused, then circled beneath him as it grew brighter.

"You liked that?" Sam whispered to the water's surface. "I'll bring you another one soon, then."

The light increased in intensity, bobbing up to the surface. Sam stared, fascinated. "You've never come this close before," he said aloud. "Maybe I'll finally get to see what you are."

He imagined any one of the numerous deep-sea fish that he'd read about, lights running along their sides to lure smaller creatures into their open maws. "What are you doing so far from home?" he mused.

A large, dark shadow passed beneath rowboat. Sam raised his eyebrow as it veered around the little light, moving quickly. Other shadows joined it, creating small waves that rocked his boat.

"That doesn't look good." He stood, trying to get a better view. More glows filtered up from the deep, this time in shades of purple instead of green.

Something made a puffing sound in the silence. Ocean spray coated his arm and Sam whirled to see where it had come from. The floorboards rocked beneath his feet, and he knelt back down, grabbing the side of the boat to steady himself.

A large black tail, like that of a giant whale, broke the water beside him. He smiled, settling back down on his seat. "Just a whale, eh? You scared me."

Another one surfaced beside him, its black and white face unlike any he'd ever seen before. It opened its mouth, almost like it was smiling hello back at him. Huge teeth lined the creature's maw.

Sam sat back in shock and grabbed his oars. "Maybe not a harmless whale, after all. It looks like it's time to get back to shore, then. I haven't seen anything with teeth like that before."

"Do you always talk to yourself when you're alone?"

"Who's there?" Sam demanded. Only the silence of the darkness answered him. "Who just said that?"

"Me." Small, feminine hands gripped the side of his boat, and a little head popped up over the edge. She was young, probably not more than eleven or twelve years old.

"What on earth are you doing out here?" Sam demanded. He grabbed her hand, ready to pull her into the boat. "There are huge fish down there. With teeth. I've never seen the like before."

"I know," she replied with a giggle. "They usually leave me alone. But they're acting strangely tonight."

"They usually leave you alone?" He stared at her, baffled. "Why are you swimming with them, and do your parents know where you are? That's dangerous."

She laughed again, a lilting melody that made him shiver. "Why don't you come find out? Swim with me."

He blinked at her. "No. You need to get in the boat so I can take you to shore. It's dangerous to come out this far, especially at night."

It was the girl's turn to stare at him, her brow wrinkled in confusion. "I don't want to go to shore. I want you to swim with me. Get in the water."

He sat back. "No. What are you? Some kind of fairy? Or have I fallen asleep and this is a dream?"

"I'm definitely not a fairy," she replied, letting go of the boat. "And I don't think you've fallen asleep, unless I have too." She glided through the water, swimming so smoothly that he couldn't even see her moving. Greenish-blue light emanated from a bauble on her wrist.

"That light... I see it very far down there occasionally."

Sam said. "Did you somehow catch it? What's it coming from?"

She smiled. "Come into the water if you want to find out. I can show you."

"I said no," he replied, getting annoyed. "I'm not playing with you, little girl. It's way past time both of us went home, so get in the boat. I can't just leave you out here."

"And I said to *get in*," the little girl demanded. She glared at him, her eyes flashing with that same eerie light that emanated from her wrist.

He picked up his oars. "I mean it. I'm leaving. Give me your hand so I can pull you in."

She gave him one last glower, then dove. He started to protest, but the words died on his lips as her long hair drifted to the side, revealing her smooth back tapering into scales.

"Wait, scales?" he said aloud. "That's impossible."

But it wasn't. Her luminous skin, shimmering in the moonlight, definitely stopped at the waist. Overlapping scales covered her form from there down, creating a long, supple fish tale, complete with wide fins at the end.

"What on earth is going on here?" he wondered aloud. She went under and he watched the little greenish-blue light- the same light he'd been tossing bits of food and other nonsense to for months - dance along the ocean's floor before disappearing for good.

Shaking his head, Sam began to row. "I must have dreamt that," he said aloud.

All at once, the water erupted around him. Black and white whales surfaced, blowing air out of the holes atop their heads, spraying him with saltwater. Sam wiped his face just in time to see the little girl come shooting out of the

water toward him, hands outstretched and terror in her
eyes.

"Help!" she screamed in panic.

One of the monstrous whales was directly behind her,
its mouth gaping open. Its teeth glistened in the moonlight,
just inches from the girl's tail fins.

Sam grabbed her wrist and hauled her aboard as he
flung an oar into the whale's mouth. It crunched down,
splintering the wood as though it were no more than a
twig.

Angry about losing the fish-girl, the monster thrashed in
the water, looking for something else to sink its teeth into.
Sam threw her against the bottom of the boat and dove on
top of her, holding her steady as the waves tossed them
about.

"What's happening?" he demanded. Cold water
splashed over the side, drenching them both as the boat
rocked violently. Sputtering, Sam sat up to see that the
whales, or whatever they were, were breaching the water's
surface, throwing their massive bodies up and crashing
down with huge splashes.

He grabbed the other oar and frantically began to row.
"We have to get out of here before they capsize us. Stay
down, and tell me what's going on!"

Helpless, she just looked up at him. "I - I have no idea.
They've never done this before," she replied. "It's like they
don't even know me."

"Know you?" he repeated as he tugged on a rope, dropping the little vessel's only sail. It caught in the wind and
began to pull them to safety, gaining speed as they rushed
toward shore. "What do you mean, know you?"

One last whale, one of the largest, chose that moment to
leap, twisting its body in the air for a heart-wrenching

moment. Sam grabbed the girl's hand and jumped, pulling her into the water with him.

The boat splintered, exploding as the monstrous animal landed right on top of it. Sam floated for a moment, paralyzed by the shockwave that reverberated through the water. The girl's fingers slipped from his hand as another whale swam beneath them, its white spots nearly glowing in the ocean's depths.

Something grabbed his hair and pulled, hard, tugging him toward the surface. The little fish girl darted around him, swimming faster than he could have imagined.

"What are you?" he tried to ask again. Water flooded his mouth, then lungs. He coughed on reflex, desperate for air.

There was none.

At least Ian's back. It's his turn to deal with the kingdom, anyway. Sam thought as his lungs burned and his vision began to fade. *Fuck, who knew drowning would be so painful?*

The wrenching pain on his scalp stopped, all of a sudden. The little girl with the blue light grabbed his arm and kept pulling, desperate to reach the shore.

It's okay, Sam tried to tell her as a whale darted at them. *Just let me go. They'll eat you before we get to the beach.*

The whale veered away, writhing in the water. Something swam around it, jabbing at it with a long stick.

Sam's head finally broke the surface as she got him to air. The little girl wrapped abnormally strong arms around his chest and squeezed, ejecting water from his lungs.

He sputtered, coughing up more seawater as he tried to suck in a breath. A wave toppled over them, forcing him back under. His arms slipped from her grip and he sank.

The little fish girl dove for him. Black and white whales circled them, weaving between them as they blocked the way to the surface.

Sam tried to swim, sluggishly pulling his arms through the water. It did no good.

Blue light suffused the water, radiating out from the little girl. Sam barely made out her face, mouth open in a strange, distorted scream that pierced his ears, even underwater.

The whales backed off for a few seconds, then came back at her.

Red light flooded the ocean this time, coming from somewhere behind Sam. The same piercing shriek sounded again, but much, much louder this time. The little girl's blue light flickered for a moment, then intensified, as though she was trying to keep up.

Something tangled in Sam's hair again, jerking him through the water as they sped toward the surface.

He didn't even care that it burned. The need for air was scorching him from the inside out.

Whales dove around them, agitated but keeping their distance. Whoever, or whatever, was pulling him slowed and thrust him toward the little girl. She snatched him up and finished the trip.

Their heads broke the surface again and Sam sucked in a deep breath. She held him up while he breathed greedily, coughing out the rest of the seawater for his efforts.

"We have to get out of here," the little fish girl hissed. "There's something wrong with the whales. And now Celeste is here, and she's going to kill me for leaving the castle. If she comes up, *do not* talk to her!"

"Why not?" Sam wheezed. "She saved us."

"Why don't you listen to anything I say?" the girl demanded. "There must be something wrong with me."

A whale came too close, flashing monstrous teeth at them only to veer back away when something - *Celeste,* Sam thought - darted into its side. Blood tinged the water in her wake.

Red scales, the color of rubies, flashed in the moonlight. Sam stared, fascinated.

She looked up and scowled.

"*Shit,*" the little girl swore. "Hold your breath."

Sam wanted to tell her to watch her mouth, but barely had time to take a deep breath before they were back underwater. She swam quickly, pulling him to the sandy shoreline.

The other girl kept pace easily, guarding them from the lingering predators. They surfaced twice more, giving Sam enough time to catch his breath before they kept going, and soon his feet were back on the ocean's floor.

He stood in waist deep water. The blue-finned girl paused beside him, settling her tail against the bottom and pushing upright on it, nearly standing as well.

"Well. I would say it's been nice meeting you, but I'm not sure that's entirely accurate," Sam managed to wheeze with a shake of his head. "Although it was definitely an adventure."

"I'm not supposed to talk to you," she whispered urgently. "Hurry up and go, before Celeste decides not to let you. No one is supposed to know about us."

The other fish girl circled them, her red light casting eerie shadows in the dark.

"But I want to say thank you," he said between coughs. "I would have died out there if it weren't for you two dragging me back to shore. What are you? How do you breathe underwater, and in the air?"

"No! You can't talk to Celeste! She'll kill you!" She ignored the rest of his questions.

Celeste came closer.

"So what am I supposed to do, just stare at her in silence?" Sam quipped in irritation. He refused to think about the threats pouring from the little girl's mouth. They had just saved him, surely this Celeste person wouldn't kill him. Right? "That sounds rude..." It hurt to talk, his throat hoarse and raw from the seawater, but he found that he didn't want to stop. He'd never seen anything like them, and the ocean had held his heart since the first time he saw it. He found himself overcome with jealousy that they lived beneath its mysterious waves.

Then Celeste surfaced and Sam found that staring in silence was quite possibly all he was capable of. She was gorgeous, in a strange sort of way.

Her dark hair streamed behind her, reaching just past her narrow shoulders as she came up beside them. Her angular face was highlighted by the dimming light that seemed to emanate from her skin. She caught his gaze and bared her teeth.

They were sharp. Almost as scary as the whales she'd saved them from. Sam was fascinated.

She can definitely take care of herself. No fainting miss here. He smiled at her in return, nearly laughing when she tilted her head in confusion.

"Thank you for saving my life. I didn't expect a simple ride in the boat to get quite so interesting this evening." He was proud that he didn't sound as dumbfounded as he felt.

Her face smoothed, losing some of the angular shape the longer she was out of the water. Sam glanced over to see that his little blue-finned companion looked positively normal now as well, albeit very pretty for a girl her age.

Normal aside from the tail, that is.

"What are you two?" he asked in wonder. *Damn it, and I was doing so well not sounding like a complete simpleton.*

Celeste bared her teeth again and grabbed the younger girl's wrist.

"No, wait -" Sam took a step forward in the water. *Just talk to me,* he wanted to beg.

They dove, lights suddenly extinguished in the swirling water. Sam thought he felt one of them brush against his leg and then they were gone, lost to the inky depths.

"This has been an exceptionally strange day."

LITTLE RED RIDING HOOD

By Nikki Dean

CHAPTER 1

The girl in red made her way through the forest, and a wolf followed.

Daphne cursed as another stick made its way through the hole in her boot, stabbing her tender flesh. She knelt to fish it out and raised her eyebrows at the giant animal tracks she found littered among the bushes.

I knew it, she thought with a flash of nervous triumph. *Now what are they up to?*

"I know you're there. You're not as sneaky as you think," she called out.

No one answered her.

"Come on now. I'll tell your alpha that you were trampling around as loud as a cow heading to its trough unless you show yourself."

A menacing growl raised the hair on her arms. "That's more like it," she said, trying to sound casual. "You're not scaring me, you know."

The growl rattled again, but in a different tone. "Maybe I should be." A man stepped out from behind the trees.

He was completely and utterly naked.

"Well, you'll certainly have to try harder than that." She mentally groaned at her own statement. *Note to self, Daphne. Don't tell naked strangers in the woods to try harder at anything.*

Daphne's hand barely shook as she slid it into her basket, wrapping her fingers around the compact crossbow that was hidden beneath her pastries.

"How did you know I was here? And how do you know my alpha?" The man cocked his head as he studied her. "Who are you?"

"You mean you don't know?" Daphne scowled. *I didn't even put on the disguise this time. I did for the others, because I thought they might recognize me from my abduction. I suppose not.* "You just stalk every woman in the woods?" The implication made her angry. "What were you planning to do with me?"

His lips twisted up into an almost-smile. "Oh, I'm still going to do it, girl. Just wait. I only shifted because you intrigued me. I was going to chase you down in my other form, but the idea that you think you'll survive this and have the chance to speak to my alpha entertained me. I get bored easily though, so the longer you stay interesting, the longer you last."

"It sounds like my lucky day," she retorted sarcastically. *He would have killed anyone walking by. Maybe I should let Ronan's pack do it their way, after all.*

"I don't know how lucky you'll think you are in a few minutes." He licked his lips as his eyes wandered down her body, pausing at her narrow hips, partially hidden beneath her voluminous red cloak. "You're a little skinny, but I'll still enjoy myself."

A little skinny, but he'll still enjoy himself? Ha. Not if I have anything to do with it. She crossed her arms in front of her chest and narrowed her eyes in exasperation. "Look here, *monsieur*. I actually had to argue with myself about *not* killing you for quite some time, but you're making me regret that effort. How about you agree to stop harassing strangers, and you just might live through the next few hours?" *Maybe. Well, probably not, actually.*

He blinked at her, taken aback. A slow grin spread over his face and he took a step forward. It only got bigger when she pulled the compact crossbow out of her basket, already loaded with a tiny bolt.

"What are you planning to do with that?" he taunted. "Toss it over so I can pick my teeth with it?"

Daphne sighed. "I know. It's ridiculous, isn't it? I prefer other means. But I did promise to try it out." She took aim and fired, shaking her head when the little arrow went wide. *I'll have to tell Papa that it's too small. Needs more weight to fly true.*

The naked wolf man burst into laughter. Much more than Daphne felt was necessarily appropriate.

"Well, as thrilling as this has been, I think it's time to get on with things," she muttered.

"I completely agree," he replied, taking a step toward her. "Although I'm surprised that you're so eager."

The werewolf licked his lips. "Or do you like it rough?"

Power surged inside her, coursing through her veins. She raised a hand to casually tuck her hair behind one ear. Vines near the stranger's feet rose up, shadowing the motion.

He growled and jumped as one brushed against his backside. Dropping into a crouch, he threw a wild look over his shoulder.

Nothing was there but the forest. A few leaves twisted in the breeze, but nothing looked out of the ordinary. Satisfied, he turned back to Daphne.

She was gone.

He looked around in confusion, unsure where she could have disappeared to. He took a deep breath, scenting the air. "You know you can't run from me, right? I can find you wherever you go."

"I'm counting on it." Her voice floated back to him from out of the woods. He grinned, a sinister twisting of his lips over sharp teeth.

The shifter dropped to all fours and transformed back into a giant wolf before taking off, leaves scattering in his wake. Daphne smiled as she watched him go, safely ensconced in the branches above. She waited several minutes before climbing down, confident that her cloaking spell would keep him from sniffing her out.

"What do you think you're doing?"

Ronan's angry hiss made her heart clench in surprised fear and she flinched. Jagged streaks of lightning erupted from her fingertips, streaking past him to hit a tree instead. Little bits of bark exploded outward, showering the ground around them.

"Don't sneak up on me like that!" she retorted, rubbing her shaking hands together. "I could have killed you!"

"Why are you out here? It's not safe by yourself." His eyes narrowed as the breeze filtered through the woods, bringing a smorgasbord of damp smells along with it. "Then again, you're not as alone as it would seem, I take it."

She scowled. "Not that it's any of your business, but no, I'm not alone. I happen to be very busy with a nice man. If you'd come upon us a few minutes earlier, you'd have even seen him naked."

Ronan's jaw tightened. Daphne couldn't help but admire the lines of his face for a moment - the dusting of a dark beard, straight nose, high cheekbones and light brown eyes that were currently narrowed at her in anger.

Humph. One would almost think he was worried, silly man. "What's wrong, darling?" She drew the endearment out. "Afraid the big, bad wolf is going to eat me? Oh wait, you already did." She pinned him with a glare of her own. "And I can't say that I was overly impressed by the experience." *But I might be persuaded to let you do it again, if only I hadn't heard you say you're thinking of taking a new mate. Blasted werewolves.*

He snorted. "I just came to tell you to be careful," he said with a growl. "We've had sightings of Voltair pack members in this area, and they're apparently very angry about something."

Daphne tossed her dishwater blonde hair over her shoulder as she cast a furtive glance around. The tree she'd hit still smoldered, the sap within it burning faster than the rain-soaked bark on the outside. There were no signs of her attacker, but Daphne bet he wasn't far away.

"It almost sounds like you're concerned for my well-being. But I know that can't be right after our last conversation." *Don't show up now,* she mentally begged the other werewolf. *I can just imagine what Ronan would say if -*

The wolf burst back into their small clearing, panting. He transformed back into a man without hesitation, running at Daphne with a snarl.

Ronan snarled back, the sound echoing through the trees as he jumped between them. Daphne cursed.

"Dammit, Ronan, move! You're blocking my shot!"

The two men crashed together, rolling across the forest floor. Daphne leaped out of the way.

Energy flared between her fingers as she took aim, trying to get a clear shot. It was impossible.

"Ronan, let him go! I can handle this by myself!" she cried out.

They grappled together, each hitting the other when an opportunity opened up. Ronan shifted, his limbs elongating and fur erupting from his body as he transformed into a massive werewolf, by far bigger than his opponent.

The other wolf man transformed as well, snapping at Ronan's legs and neck. Ronan returned in kind and soon blood dripped from them both.

Daphne glowered. She lifted her hands as she whispered a spell and vines sprang up around them, pulling the two beasts apart. Ronan growled in fury as she pinned the first wolf, then Ronan, securely to the ground.

"I told you I had this." She set her hands on her hips and glared down at him. "Why did you get in the way?"

He transformed back into a human. A very naked human.

Don't think about it, don't think about it, don't think about it, Daphne told herself. *If he doesn't care, I don't care.* The barest hint of pink stained her cheeks anyway.

"What the hell is going on here?" he demanded. "Let me go!"

A flash of memory revealed him laid out on his back in the woods, vines wrapped around his wrists in a not-so-dissimilar fashion, but completely different circumstances. Recalling the way he'd looked, tied down as she rode him had her blushing a little more. Daphne prayed that he didn't see.

"Daphne."

The vines tightened by a fraction before they fell away, brown and withering. She turned from him without answering.

"Daphne." Something else threaded through his voice

beneath the anger. She still didn't respond, instead walking over to the other wolf that still thrashed against his bonds.

She waited. His body rippled, then shrank as he shifted back into human form. "Just wait until I get my hands on you, you bitch. I'm going to make you pay -"

"Enjoy this, bastard." Electricity shot from her fingers for the second time that day, blasting him in the chest. His eyes bulged as his body was forced into the dirt, making a crater around him before he passed out.

"Anton Voltair," she said without looking back. "Do whatever you want with him. My job is done."

Ronan raised an eyebrow in surprise. "Voltair? That's what you're doing out here? Killing the Voltairs?" *I never would have imagined*, he thought with a grudging smidge of respect. *But I should have. She's always up to something, especially if it means finding Granny Rousseau. I'm sure the Voltairs, or someone with them, abducted her, but we have no proof.*

Not really related to any of them, the old enchantress had been a fixture in her cottage at Macconde Falls. She'd taken in wandering wolf cubs and the occasional lost child alike over the years, earning her the universal title of "Granny". Ronan had grown up running in and out of her cottage, listening to her stories about magic and playing with her conjured creatures. Daphne had only met her recently though, when she agreed to be Granny's apprentice. Now Granny was gone, and Daphne was a formidable enchantress on her own, determined to rescue the old lady.

"No. I'm just capturing them, and leaving them on your pack's land. You get to kill them if you want. Did you get my last three?"

"We've been wondering why Voltair pack members would be in our territory. Claude found two of them while he was out on patrol. We questioned them, but didn't get any useful information. Neither of them mentioned you."

"Of course not. I told them that I would skin them alive if they did."

He came up behind her, so close that she could feel the heat radiating from his bare chest. She had to resist the urge to lean back against him, to see if he'd wrap his strong arms around her like before. If he'd hold her like she actually meant something to him.

"Daph..." He set his hand against her shoulder blade.

She forced herself to move away. "Let me know what you find out from him. If anything. What have you been doing with the others?"

"The usual," he answered after a brief hesitation. "I have to give them an opportunity to join the pack."

She bristled.

"But none of them have, so we've done challenges instead."

"Who fights?"

"Me, of course."

Her chest tightened and she looked down at her hands. Studying them. "Well, I suppose it hasn't been too bad then. You seem fine."

"No thanks to you."

The words were almost too quiet for Daphne's human ears to hear. She whirled in outrage.

"Look, I understand what you're trying to do, but it's not worth your life. He could have killed you, Daph. Any of them could have."

"And yet, they didn't," she retorted in anger. "Because they, like you, completely underestimate me."

"I don't underestimate you," he said between clenched teeth.

"Oh, really? What do you call it then?"

"I just worry about you. You should be with the pack, at least until we find Granny Rousseau. You can have your own place - I won't bother you at all." He tried to make that last part sound believable, like he could fight the draw to be near her. It worked.

Of course you wouldn't bother me. That would be too much effort for you, she thought angrily. "Don't worry about me, I'm just the babysitter. Remember?"

The werewolf on the ground in front of them groaned as his eyelids fluttered. Daphne shot him again, then walked away. The vines withered behind her, freeing his body for Ronan to deal with.

"I miss you," he said softly. Too softly. She disappeared in the underbrush, never once looking back.

UNTITLED

Well, that's it for Belle and her Beast for now! They'll still pop up from time to time in the rest of the Frisky Fairy Tales series, and might get their own short stories as well, since they are my favorite and I just can't let them go. I love them too much to stop playing with them entirely, but for now, their story is done. Thank you so much for reading my version. I hope you enjoyed it, and look forward to hearing what you thought in a review, which will help other like-minded readers find and enjoy the book too!

Please join my mailing list at http://eepurl.com/cn3wqn for information on new releases. I promise not to bombard you with junk mail or sell your information under any circumstances. I do offer exclusive scenes and short stories to my newsletter readers from time to time.

I can be found on Facebook at https://www.facebook.com/Nikki-Deans-Naughty-Tales-381074525571165/ Thanks again for reading!

Made in the USA
Middletown, DE
30 August 2023